Hide and GEEK

By T. P. Jagger

HIDE AND GEEK
Hide and Geek
The Treasure Test

HIDE AND GEEK

T. P. Jagger

A YEARLING BOOK

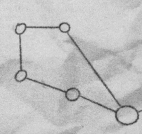

This is a work of fiction. Names, characters, places, and incidents either
are the product of the author's imagination or are used fictitiously. Any resemblance
to actual persons, living or dead, events, or locales is entirely coincidental.

Text copyright © 2022 by Working Partners Ltd.
Cover art copyright © 2022 by Chris Danger

All rights reserved. Published in the United States by Yearling, an imprint of
Random House Children's Books, a division of Penguin Random House LLC, New York.
Originally published in hardcover in the United States by Random House
Children's Books, a division of Penguin Random House LLC, New York, in 2022.

Yearling and the jumping horse design
are registered trademarks of Penguin Random House LLC.

Visit us on the Web! rhcbooks.com

Educators and librarians, for a variety of teaching tools,
visit us at RHTeachersLibrarians.com

The Library of Congress has cataloged the hardcover edition of this work as follows:
Names: Jagger, T. P., author.
Title: Hide and GEEK / T. P. Jagger.
Description: New York: Random House Children's Books, 2022.
Summary: Eleven-year-old Gina Sparks, aspiring journalist, and her fellow
GEEKs, Edgar, Elena, and Kevin, live in Elmwood, New Hampshire, a small
town in serious danger of vanishing completely—unless the four friends can find
the Van Houten fortune, which was supposedly promised to the town by
Maxine Van Houten, a famous toymaker who loved complicated puzzles.
Identifiers: LCCN 2021005586 | ISBN 978-0-593-37793-2 (hc) |
ISBN 978-0-593-37794-9 (lib. bdg.) | ISBN 978-0-593-37832-8 (ebook)
Subjects: LCSH: Treasure troves—Juvenile fiction. | Inheritance and succession—Juvenile
fiction. | Toymakers—Juvenile fiction. | Best friends—Juvenile fiction. | Cities and towns—
New Hampshire—Economic conditions—Juvenile fiction. | Detective and mystery stories. |
New Hampshire—Juvenile fiction. | CYAC: Mystery and detective stories. |
Buried treasure—Fiction. | Inheritance and succession—Fiction. | Toymakers—Fiction. |
Best friends—Fiction. | Friendship—Fiction. | Cities and towns—Fiction. |
New Hampshire—Fiction. | LCGFT: Detective and mystery fiction.
Classification: LCC PZ7.1.J38445 Hi 2022 | DDC 813.6 [Fic]—dc23

ISBN 978-0-593-37795-6 (pbk.)

Printed in the United States of America
10 9 8 7 6 5 4 3 2 1
First Yearling Edition 2023

Random House Children's Books supports the First Amendment
and celebrates the right to read.

For Amy—
because you said yes

PROLOGUE

Okay, by now I'm sure you've heard about everything going on in the tiny town of Elmwood, New Hampshire, tucked away in the scenic Fair Valley. You've read the headlines or seen the photos or whatever. The failing factory, the hidden fortune, the kidnappings, all that stuff.

Last week, a reporter showed up all the way from Australia to get the scoop. Unfortunately, except for his cool accent, he was like every other person who's flooded into Elmwood lately—chasing a fairy tale. But me? I grew up in Elmwood, and I care about the facts. So before you judge me for not *looking* like a journalist, consider this:

FACT #1: Girls usually have their growth spurts between ten and fourteen years old.

1

FACT #2: I'm only eleven, so I have another three years. I could totally grow past 4'6" any day now.

Anyway, I may be a short, freckle-faced eleven-year-old, but I'm here to set the record straight, to take a stand for truth. After all, I'm not simply reporting what I *think* happened in Elmwood. I'm Gina Sparks, soon-to-be-world-famous journalist, and I was there. I lived through it. Barely. And facts are what saved my life.

Well, facts plus one little lie about Mark Twain.

I realize you kind of already know how the story ends. At least you think you do. But as with all good stories, the best place to start is at the beginning. Or, if not quite at the beginning, at least at the part of the story where someone dies.

The Elmwood Tribune

Friday, August 20

LAST VAN HOUTEN IN ELMWOOD
FOUND DEAD IN ROCKING CHAIR

By GINA SPARKS
(First Draft)

No paintball attacks have been reported on Scrub-stone Lane since local recluse Alice Van Houten passed away recently at the age of 94. [*This is a clear and catchy lede, Gina Bean. Good job!*] Although the exact time of her death is unknown, her body was discovered on Wednesday, August 18, by mailman Frank Nubbins. Mr. Nubbins spotted Ms. Van Houten seated peacefully in her rocking chair on the front porch of Van Houten Manor. When she failed to yell at him or fire paintballs to chase him off her property, he decided to investigate. The classic Van Houten Bazooka Boom-Painter 2000 on Ms. Van Houten's lap was still loaded with a neon-orange paintball grenade. Police Chief Luis Hernández has confirmed that the cause of Ms. Van Houten's death was simply "being a really old lady."

Ms. Van Houten was the eldest and last surviving child of famous local toy maker Maxine Van Houten. As a female pioneer in both engineering design and business, Maxine was best known for inventing the internationally acclaimed 3D puzzle the Bamboozler, produced by her Van Houten Toy & Game Company. Of course, Maxine was also known for her public promises to leave the bulk of her fortune to the town of Elmwood. ~~That ended up being a total lie.~~ **However, after Maxine's death, the Van Houten fortune was never given to the town—instead, it disappeared.** It is believed that Maxine's frequent, unexplained absences from Elmwood prior to her death may have been for secret trips to Foxwoods Casino, where she is thought to have squandered her fortune on bingo. Ever since Maxine's death on April 3, 1987, her ~~greedy~~ children have ~~neglected~~ **turned their attentions away from** their mother's company, eventually selling off the Bamboozler to a rival company, ~~gutting our great town's heart and crushing~~ **seriously affecting** the local economy.

Ms. Alice Van Houten spent the last few decades alone on the family's estate. It is rumored that the peculiar crashing and banging noises often reported by locals passing the now-crumbling manor were in fact Ms. Van Houten searching futilely for her mother's lost fortune and ~~going a bit batty~~ **losing touch with reality** in the process. ~~If these rumors are true, they kind of served Ms. Van Houten right, considering the way her family treated our town.~~ [*Be nice, Bean.*]

4

Ms. Van Houten was preceded in death by her parents, Maxine and Harold Van Houten; younger siblings Cynthia Van Houten and Harold Van Houten, Jr.; and five different cats—Otis, Otis, Otis, Otis, and Otis. She is survived by her nephew—Maxwell Van Houten—and by her 14-year-old tortoiseshell cat, Otis.

If you are interested in becoming the caretaker for a ~~grumpy old cat that constantly hacks up hairballs~~ **mature cat with special dietary needs,** please contact the Van Houten estate, care of Mr. Thomas Ridley, Attorney-at-Law. A two-month supply of Feline Queen Salmon Supreme Hairball Control canned cat food is included.

No public memorial service will be held for Ms. Van Houten, and the fate of Van Houten Manor is not yet known.

[This is a good first draft, Bean, but don't let your personal connection to the news interfere with your ability to report without bias. Remember, a reporter must remain objective, even if she has strong feelings about her subject. —Mom]

I may not be a math genius like my friend Kevin, but I can count. And because I'm a journalist, it's important for me to record things accurately, which is why I always keep a pencil tucked into my bun and carry my scuffed-up leather notebook (it's vintage—a birthday gift from Mom last year). So when Kevin popped from his lunchroom seat like a jack-in-the-box, I knew it was the twenty-seventh time he'd done that in only eight minutes.

"Kevin Robinson for president! Be sure to vote!" Kevin blurted. He snatched a KEVIN FOR SIXTH-GRADE CLASS PRESIDENT flyer from the massive stack in the middle of our lunch table and thrust it toward Gunner Bradley, who nearly dropped his lunch tray in surprise. "Scientific calculators for every student and new science-lab equipment! More funding for the debate team and educational field trips! Help *me* help *you* make Elmwood Middle School a better place to learn!"

Instead of the outstretched flyer, Gunner snatched a chicken nugget from Kevin's lunch and said, "Thanks, dude. Chicken nuggets rule!"

As Gunner hustled away, I glanced across the lunch table at my other two best friends—Edgar Feingarten and Elena Hernández. Elena and I shared an eye roll. Kevin had been class president in third grade, in fourth grade, and in fifth. *Of course* he'd be class president again in sixth grade. Nobody else ever bothered to run against him. Plus, he was the one who'd started the school's peer-tutoring program, raised money for new sports equipment with a car wash, and got the cafeteria to turn the smelly lunch scraps into compost for the school garden. He had good ideas, and everyone knew it.

Kevin sat down and smoothed the flyer on the edge of the table. He rubbed at the collar of his polo shirt. "Do you think I need a tie? To look more presidential?"

"Mmm," Edgar grunted, his round face buried in some new play script. As he read, he unconsciously played with his hair, twisting and untwisting one of his loopy red curls.

Elena took a swig of chocolate milk. "What you need, Kev, is a classier look. Like mine." Elena ran her hands down her wrinkled T-shirt, which had a picture of Albert Einstein on the front. Einstein's hair shot out in all directions, in contrast to Elena's, which her abuela braided nice and tight and neat every morning before school.

Kevin shook his head. "I'm serious, Elena. Class president is an important position. I'd be able to make this school better for *everyone*. I could help improve our educational outcomes and experiences. I can't just—"

"He can't just slap up a few posters and call it a campaign." An all-too-unwelcome voice cut in. Silver bracelets jangled on Sophina Burkhart's wrist as she reached over Kevin's shoulder and plucked up a flyer. Glittery polish flashed on her perfectly manicured nails as she brushed back a strand of her shoulder-length, straight blond hair. Sophina's trailing pack of minions—Kyesha Killman, Bella Ronelli-Compelli, and Mandy Sykes—all peered over her shoulder. "This year, Kevin will actually have to *earn* his votes."

"I—I can get votes," Kevin spluttered. "I have ideas. Experience."

"Sure you do," Sophina said. She studied Kevin's flyer before casually tossing it back onto the table. Her green eyes sparkled. "But why would anyone vote for you . . . when they can vote for *me*?"

Kevin's dark eyes widened. "I—what—you?" he stammered. He tugged at the collar of his shirt. If Sophina was being serious, this was not good. Like Kevin, Sophina was smart. *Unlike* Kevin, she was also popular.

Without turning around, Sophina held a hand over one shoulder. Mandy Sykes passed her a sheet of paper. "See for yourself," Sophina said, dropping the paper on top of Kevin's flyers.

Kevin stared, speechless. The paper said VOTE SOPHINA at the top, followed by a list of campaign promises.

"Don't worry, Kevin," Sophina said. "I'm sure Gina, Edgar, and Elena will still vote for—" She stopped and stifled a giggle. "You know what? I just realized something. Gina, Edgar, Elena, Kevin. *G-E-E-K*. Together, you are—*literally*—GEEKs."

Sophina's minions laughed. My cheeks grew hot. I couldn't believe none of *us* had ever noticed our initials before.

Sophina gave a satisfied grin before sticking her chin in the air and spinning away. "See you later . . . *GEEKs.*"

Elena made a little growling noise. "She'll be sorry."

"Don't do it, Elena," I said. "Whatever you're thinking—don't do it."

Elena batted her eyelashes innocently. "Who, me? Why, I wasn't thinking anything. Maybe just a tiny, harmless prank is in her future, that's all."

"Yeah right, Elena," Edgar said. "Everybody knows there's nothing tiny about your pranks. They tend to be of the epic variety." The time she'd somehow filled the locker room with bath bubbles sprang to mind. And there'd been an unfortunate incident involving exploding ketchup bottles and Principal Gawkmeyer's favorite sweater. "Come on," Edgar continued. "The science thing, remember?"

Elena had been accepted into an amazing weeklong science program over winter break, but her dad would only let her go if she stayed out of trouble until then. Her jaw clenched and her nostrils flared. But she took a slow, deep breath. "Particle-accelerator tour," she chanted to herself. "Personalized lab coats."

Sophina and her minions pranced away, handing out campaign flyers and calling, "Vote for Sophina Burkhart! Sophina for sixth-grade class president!"

"Also, be sure to enjoy a free cake pop after school!" Sophina added. "Courtesy of Burkhart Bakery!"

Shouts and cheers erupted around the lunchroom.

Kevin drooped in his seat. He ran a hand nervously across the tight black curls of his high-top fade. "I'm totally doomed. . . ."

"Come on, Kevin," Edgar said. "It's not that bad."

"Not that bad? Look at this!" He shook Sophina's campaign flyer. "High-gloss, premium heavyweight paper. Color laser printing. Campaign promises I'll never be able to compete against!"

"Hmm," I said. I tapped my pencil against the flyer. "Her 'no homework' promise *does* seem newsworthy. . . ."

"This is serious, Gina!" Kevin wailed. "Who's going to vote for me when Sophina's promising a schoolwide no-homework policy, plus being allowed to text in class? There's no way she could deliver those things, but all she needs is for enough kids to *believe* she can."

"Jeez, Kev," Elena said. She swiped a chicken nugget through the pool of ketchup on her lunch tray, then pointed it toward Kevin. "Edge is the actor, but you're the one with all the drama."

"And anyway," I said, "Sophina may have cake pops, but the fact is, nobody has more experience than you do. You've got a proven track record."

Kevin started shaking his head before I'd even finished talking. "Maybe. But here's another fact—Sophina's popular, while I'm just a . . . a geek."

"Hey, there's nothing wrong with being a geek," I said, although I shuddered slightly at the thought of our new GEEKs label being passed around the cafeteria as we spoke.

"And if Sophina gets everybody mocking us for being geeks, what will happen in a few years?" Kevin said. "The bullies are bigger in high school, and when you get stuffed in a gym locker, it'll smell worse."

"If some high school punk tries to stuff *me* into a

locker, he'll get more than he bargained for." Elena rubbed her hands together, her eyes sparkling. "A little decarboxylated lysine through his locker slats would teach him to be more careful who he messed with."

"De-car-box-a-what?" Edgar asked.

"Decarboxylated lysine," Elena said. "Basically, roadkill perfume. Great stuff."

"Wow," I said. "I'm sure glad you're my geeky friend, not my geeky enemy."

Elena lobbed a soggy French fry at my head.

"At least the high school has a real theater program," Edgar said. He waved his script around. "How am I ever going to get my name in lights on Broadway when I'm stuck in a middle school drama club that only has three members?" Edgar added a deep sigh, but we knew it was part of his act. For all his talk about becoming a famous Broadway actor, he loved Elmwood too much to leave. Plus, he was destined to be an Elmwood lifer, no matter what. Because there are two important facts you should know about Edgar Feingarten:

FACT #1: He's the only child of New Hampshire dairy farmers.

FACT #2: He's loyal.

Edgar would never let himself be the one who removed the *family* from Feingarten Family Farms.

Plus, he'd never be able to abandon his favorite prizewinning heifer, Ollie.

I turned to Kevin. "Elmwood Middle needs you." I picked up Sophina's campaign flyer and crumpled it into a ball. "So you can't let Sophina bully you out of running."

"You're right." Kevin sat up a little straighter. "Hey, if I win, will your mom put me on the front page of the paper?"

I slid my pencil back into my hair bun. "It's possible." But I felt an uncomfortable twinge in my stomach that I couldn't blame on the cafeteria food. The *Elmwood Tribune* had deep roots in the town, but subscriptions had been falling for four straight years. We'd had a bit of a sales bump after Alice Van Houten died (thanks in part, I like to think, to the obituary I'd written as my first official assignment). But it hadn't lasted.

Mom and I had both been on the lookout nonstop for the next big scoop. Or even a medium scoop. Really, any scoop would do. But printing the results of the middle school's class elections wasn't likely to help much.

At least Kevin was a bit more hopeful now. "This school is too important to have a class president who isn't completely prepared for the job. I can't let Sophina ruin my campaign."

Elena clapped him on the shoulder and whooped, "Go get 'em, Kev!"

"But for now . . ." Kevin glanced up at the cafeteria clock. "Only two minutes until the bell rings. We really need to get to our next classes."

"Aha! The importance of getting to class," Edgar said. He stabbed a finger into the air. "That's the way of the GEEKs!" Then, seeing the look on all our faces, he shrugged. "What? If we can't escape it, we might as well embrace it."

And, just like that, we were no longer simply geeks. We were *the* GEEKs.

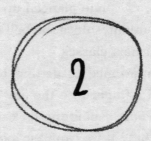

2

There are three important facts about last-period social studies that make it the best class of the day:

FACT #1: Other than lunch, social studies is the only period with all four GEEKs.

FACT #2: Edgar, Elena, Kevin, and I sit together in the front row.

FACT #3: Our teacher, Mr. Singh, likes bow ties, blue jeans, and socks with sandals. And he *doesn't* like to style his overgrown mustache the same way two days in a row. He's pretty consistently entertaining. (Okay, that last bit was an opinion.)

"As we shall learn during our next unit," Mr. Singh said near the end of class that afternoon, "the late eighteenth century was a time of revolution. Of upheaval, social change, and, *oui*—bloodshed."

Edgar leaned over his desk and whispered, "It also happens to be part of two of the best musicals of all time, *Les Misérables* and—"

"*Hamilton*," I finished. "I know, I know." Edgar had memorized both entire cast albums and sang them whenever he wasn't busy quoting Shakespeare or whatever play he was reading at the time.

I jumped when Mr. Singh plopped something heavy on his desk and announced in a terrible French accent: "I give you—*une petite guillotine!*"

We all leaned forward as Mr. Singh produced a watermelon from under his desk. His mustache—which today looked like he'd glued a pair of squirrel tails to the middle of his face—twitched as he placed the melon under the guillotine's blade. "During the French Revolution, both aristocrats and common criminals met their demise by the blade of this device, which I will now demonstrate." Mr. Singh winked as he pulled a thin rope to raise the blade of the miniature guillotine. "I hope you're all hungry."

The class cheered.

However, before Mr. Singh could release the blade, a beep and a crackle sounded from the speaker mounted above the classroom door.

The class booed.

"Attention, educators. Attention, scholars," Principal Gawkmeyer wheezed through the intercom. "I apologize for this interruption. However, I have an important announcement. I just received notification that the town's select board has scheduled an emergency town meeting."

Huh? Elmwood *never* had town meetings. I opened my notebook and pulled the pencil from my hair bun. Kevin's mom was on the select board, so I glanced his way and silently mouthed, *What's it about?*

Kevin pursed his lips and shrugged.

Principal Gawkmeyer continued: "The meeting is scheduled for seven o'clock this evening at the Elmwood Town Hall. Scholars, please inform your parents. I hope to see them tonight. Thank you."

As soon as the intercom clicked off, the rest of the class forgot all about the announcement. A chant of "Wa-ter-me-lon! Wa-ter-me-lon!" filled the room.

Mr. Singh once again prepared to release the guillotine's blade.

The end-of-day bell clanged.

"Alas," Mr. Singh said, stepping back from the guillotine, arms raised. "The execution has been postponed."

The class groaned.

Mr. Singh scooped the watermelon into his arms and cradled it like a baby. "Worry not, *mes amis.* On Monday, this felonious fruit shall receive its just deserts. Then you shall receive your desserts as well!"

I half smiled at Mr. Singh's attempt at humor. But as I followed the flow of students out the door, my mind spun around the emergency town meeting, my reporter radar pinging. The newspaper needed a scoop, and now it looked like there might be one.

Unfortunately, it's like they always say—be careful what you wish for.

3

Everyone should know the difference between facts and opinions, but it's especially important for a journalist. And the fact is this—my friends and I had different opinions about the town meeting.

> **OPINION #1:** Go. "It's our civic duty, guys. We *have* to go. Participation in the democratic process is vital for a successful government!" (Kevin)

> **OPINION #2:** Don't go. "Seriously? You've gotta be kidding, Kev. It's gonna be *soooo* boring. . . ." (Elena)

> **OPINION #3:** Don't go. "I have chores to do. Besides, I told Ollie we would finish the *Wicked* cast album this afternoon!" (Edgar, mistaking his heifer for a fellow musical-theater fan)

OPINION #4: Go. "It could be breaking news, and I'm a journalist. I have to be there!" (Me, obviously)

We stood outside the school, arguing back and forth—two votes to go, two votes to skip—until Elena eventually said, "If we skip the meeting and go to the Lookout, I'll bring some of my abuela's taquitos *and* her chocolate chip cookies."

"No fair," Kevin protested. "You can't—"

"I call a vote. Boring town meeting or taquitos and cookies?"

My mouth watered. Once a month, Elena's grandma makes taquitos with crunchy homemade tortillas and the tenderest, most mouthwatering meat you've ever tasted. In other words, she makes the best taquitos in the world. They can be outdone only by her chocolate chip cookies, which are the best in the *universe*. Mom would be at the meeting, after all. Maybe two world-class journalists covering one town hall meeting would be overkill. . . .

Kevin lost the vote three to one.

Kevin moaned. "You just undermined the entire democratic process." But then he checked his watch. "Debate team starts in ten minutes. I guess I'll see you guys at the Lookout at seven o'clock."

"I have to go too," Edgar said. "Drama club."

"And I've gotta get some stuff done in the lab," Elena said with a wave.

Just like that, I stood alone outside Elmwood Middle School. I didn't mind. Edgar, Elena, and Kevin had talents that came with clubs and rehearsals and spotlights and awards. I was used to being the observer, the one hanging out in the background. For a journalist, the background is a very useful place to be.

I hopped on my bike and headed home. (And, yes, my bike has a basket attached to the handlebars. As any too-young-to-drive journalist knows, it's the perfect spot to keep a notebook when pedaling around town, hunting for news.)

Anyway, for me, heading *home* isn't quite the same as it is for most kids. That's because my mom and I live in an apartment above the office of the *Elmwood Tribune*. In fact, our kitchen used to be the newspaper's break room back when the paper had more staff than just me and my mom. My tiny bedroom still has a brass plaque on the door that reads OPINION EDITOR.

The newspaper office is on the outskirts of town, but Elmwood isn't that big, so it was a quick ride. Plus, I pumped my legs a bit harder than usual, my bike creaking with every push of the pedals. I couldn't wait to see if Mom knew anything about the town meeting.

As soon as I got to the office, I let my bike clatter to the ground beside the crumbling redbrick building, which had THE ELMWOOD TRIBUNE stenciled on the dusty front window in peeling black-and-gold paint. I bounded inside. My mom sat at her desk, forehead resting in her hands, staring at some papers.

"Hey, Mom!" I called out.

Her head whipped up. "Gina!" she gasped. She flung a file folder over the papers in front of her, but I spotted two words stamped across the top paper before she could cover them up. Bold, red letters declared: FINAL NOTICE.

I felt a pit in my stomach. *Final notice?* I wondered. *Of what?*

My gaze wandered around the newspaper office. My mom's cluttered desk. The stacks of old newspapers. The floor-to-ceiling shelves filled with classic books Mom and I had read together over the years: *The Birchbark House* . . . *Where the Red Fern Grows* . . . *Oliver Twist.* And, on the top shelf, a glass case holding an American flag, folded into a tight triangle and given to my mom when she was pregnant with me. A gift from the United States Coast Guard. Presented at the funeral of Lieutenant Joseph "J. T." Sparks—the dad I never got to meet.

I let out a slow breath, then inhaled the ever-present smell of printer's ink and newsprint. What would my life be like without the *Elmwood Tribune* . . . without my *home*? What if—

"How was school, Gina Bean?" Mom asked, using the nickname I'd had since I was a baby. She gave a flustered smile. Her eyes flicked briefly to the top of her desk. She shifted the folder to the side, sliding the hidden papers along with it.

"School was fine," I said, trying not to let my worry show. "Have you heard about the meeting at the town hall?"

"Yes, Kevin's mom called."

"What's it about?"

Mom shook her head. "She wouldn't say. I'll have to find out with everyone else at seven o'clock." A worried look clouded her face like a smear of ink on a misprinted newspaper sheet. Then she forced a smile, which didn't quite make it past her cheeks. "In the meantime, can I get you to swing by the Maple Leaf? Mrs. Dupree has money for last month's papers. I thought you could collect the payment while I . . ." Mom's eyes drifted toward the folder on her desk. Her shoulders tensed. "While I wrap up a few things here."

My fingers twitched. I wanted to snatch the file folder and inspect whatever hid beneath it. Instead I stuffed my hands into the front pouch of my sweatshirt. "Okay," I said. "And you'll have to tell me all about tonight's meeting later. Elena, Edgar, Kevin, and I are planning to hang out. Is that okay?"

"Sure, Bean." Mom's shoulders relaxed slightly. "And thanks. Now, don't forget your phone."

"Got it," I said, grabbing my cell from my backpack. I also tugged out my notebook with its clip-on reading light and double-checked my hair bun for my pencil. While I was out, I could observe, take notes, look for leads. Anything that might help the paper. Anything that might erase the two words hidden on Mom's desk but stamped in red ink across my brain: FINAL NOTICE.

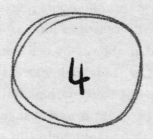

4

I've already told you a lot about me—who my friends are, what my mom does, how much I love journalism. One thing I *haven't* talked about yet is Sauce. Here are some facts:

FACT #1: Sauce is my dog—50 percent basset hound, 50 percent Scottish terrier, 100 percent adorable (okay . . . those facts are based on the opinion of our vet, Dr. Langhofer, but she's a smart doctor).

FACT #2: I found him in the alley behind the Maple Leaf General Store and Diner when he was a puppy, pawing at an empty jar of Sweet Mountain Mama's Honey Maple Barbecue Sauce, which had gotten stuck over his snout.

FACT #3: Once I freed him from the jar, he covered my face in kisses—and sauce. The rest is history.

Nowadays, Sauce never misses a chance to revisit the Maple Leaf, where it seems like a hamburger patty always "falls off the grill" right when he shows up. I went to get him before heading into town.

As usual, I found Sauce back in the printing room, snuggled onto the nest of old newspapers piled between the printing press and the metal stairs leading up to our apartment. His basset-hound ears flopped out from the sides of his head, resting on the floor like a pair of furry wings. His Scottish-terrier mustache spread out on the newspapers in front of his nose like the whiskers on a walrus. He was snoring.

"Hey, Sauce! Wake up, boy!" I gave him a quick scratch between the ears.

He didn't move.

"Wanna go into town?"

Still nothing.

"Wanna visit Mrs. Dupree?"

Sauce's eyes shot open. He scrambled to his feet and started galumphing around in circles, his stubby legs pitter-pattering across the cement floor. With a single happy howl, he licked me across the kneecap and barged out his doggy door in a white-and-brown jumble of fur.

"Sauce!" I grabbed his leash and a fistful of doggy biscuits from a nearby bin and charged after him. "Come back!"

Sauce was a hundred yards down White Bend Road before I finally caught up on my bike.

"Bad dog," I scolded as I pedaled up beside him, but my heart wasn't in it, and Sauce ignored me anyway. I fixed his leash to his collar, and we cruised toward town together, me pedaling, Sauce chugging along in his short-legged gallop. The squeak of my bike's rusty chain was accompanied by the patter of Sauce's paws and the flap of his ears. His long, low stomach nearly dragged along the road as he ran.

It was a clear, sunny September day, but the air was cool, and trees shadowed most of our route. We passed the Van Houten Nature Conservatory, where pine trees mixed with the towering oaks and birches, whose colors were just beginning to turn to their fall kaleidoscope of reds and yellows and oranges. The nature preserve began on the east side of Elmwood, wrapped around the entire southern part of the town, and passed behind Elmwood Elementary and Elmwood Middle, ending when it butted up against the back side of the Van Houten estate on the western edge of town. On its other side, it was bordered by the White Bend River, which separated Elmwood from its closest neighbor, Grove

Park. The preserve provided homes for white-tailed deer and wild turkeys and loads of other animals. It also housed a deserted, decaying observation tower, which Elena, Edgar, Kevin, and I had dubbed the Lookout. It was our go-to spot when we wanted to get together and talk (or eat taquitos and cookies) in private.

After the preserve, Sauce and I passed by redbrick houses and clapboard cottages, some of them neat and clean and tidy, but too many others with collapsed picket fences, sagging porches, and FOR SALE signs planted in overgrown lawns. Then, finally, we arrived in the heart of Elmwood, where I soaked in the familiar sights of the town I had always called home.

White Bend Road was one of four main roads that led into downtown like the lines of a tic-tac-toe board, with the town square sitting in the board's center. The square featured the fire and police stations, Elmwood Community Church, and a variety of shops, including the Maple Leaf and Emily's Antiques. There was also the town hall, with its arched doorway declaring ELMWOOD— FOUNDED JULY 2, 1779. Beside the town hall stood a building with tall white pillars out front and a dome rising from the middle of the otherwise flat roof. It used to be a Premier Mutual bank, but the building had been abandoned so long that hardly any proof of that remained. Even the sign declaring its name had been worn away.

We GEEKs just called it the Capitol, because it looked like a miniature version of the Capitol building in Washington, DC.

And, finally, one entire side of the square was devoted to the Elmwood Theater. The theater was once state-of-the-art, but a fire in downtown Elmwood in the 1980s was followed by decades of neglect. Now the theater's bricks were chipped, and black soot still stained the walls around its boarded-up windows.

All these buildings boxed in Van Houten Park, where the gazebo drooped and the flower garden was a tangle of overgrown rosebushes and weeds. In the middle of the park stood a larger-than-life bronze statue of Maxine Van Houten herself, with a model of a Bamboozler tucked under one arm. Once upon a time, Maxine's statue even had one hand raised in a friendly wave, but the arm busted off years ago, like it was too tired to actually hold its own greeting.

Even though Van Houten Park was a run-down wreck, it was easy to imagine what it *used* to be. What it one day, once again, *could* be. I could picture the gazebo with a fresh coat of white paint, its latticework repaired, red-white-and-blue streamers decorating it every Fourth of July. I could smell the flower garden, bursting with spring blooms. I could even imagine Maxine Van Houten with a new arm.

When Sauce and I arrived in downtown Elmwood,

we didn't head straight for the Maple Leaf to see Mrs. Dupree. Instead I drew a doggy biscuit from my pocket and bribed Sauce into following me into the park. Along with loving hamburgers, Sauce is a big fan of stink. He was soon snuffling the ground for anything rotten or otherwise smelly.

I leaned my bike against the base of Maxine's statue and grabbed my notebook from the basket. I climbed up and perched against the statue's legs, pulled the pencil from my hair bun, and settled in for a few minutes of "observations and cogitations," which my mom taught me is a fancy way to say I'm looking for facts and also thinking about them. After all, a good journalist can't just *find* facts. She has to draw connections and make sense of them.

I listened to the voices of the Elmwood Community Church choir spilling through the church's open doors. Not news. I caught the whiff of fresh bread coming from Burkhart Bakery. Not news. I witnessed old Ms. Lavoie shuffle through the park's flower garden and snip off a half-wilted rose. Spotted the fire chief tilted back in a chair outside the Elmwood Fire Department. Watched a couple of preschoolers dig for worms at the base of a maple tree as their mothers chatted nearby. Not news. Not news. Not news.

Then the front door to the office of Thomas Ridley, Attorney-at-Law, swung outward.

My reporter radar pinged as soon as the stranger strolled from Mr. Ridley's office.

Elmwood is a small town with few visitors. And when folks *do* visit, they aren't usually making social calls to Elmwood's only lawyer. I sat up straighter. My heartbeat quickened. I tightened my grip on my pencil. *This* looked like news. Or at least a lead . . .

The man walking out of Mr. Ridley's office was slight, with thinning brown hair slicked back from his forehead. He wore a charcoal-gray suit with a shiny blue tie, and even from my perch in the park, his black leather shoes looked freshly polished. He clutched a large yellow envelope to his chest along with a ring of keys. When the stranger cut across the park, heading toward Scrubstone Lane, I hopped from the statue to follow him.

"Come on, boy," I told Sauce. "Time for some investigative reporting."

But just as we started to slink through the park's flower garden, something caught Sauce's attention that was more important to him than a front-page exclusive.

"Gina! Sauce!" a familiar voice sang out. "Good afternoon!"

Even though I had Sauce on a leash, my grip is no match for him when he senses a hamburger coming. He bolted, and the leash whipped out of my hand.

"No, Sauce!" I yelled. "Not yet! Want another biscuit?"

Too late. Sauce bounded across the street (good thing there's hardly any traffic in downtown Elmwood) and threw himself at Mrs. Dupree's knees, tail wagging. I gave one final glance toward the gray-suited stranger as he disappeared around the corner by Burkhart Bakery.

My shoulders slumped. Why did Sauce's nose for news have to be so easily undone by hamburgers? With a sigh, I crossed the street to the Maple Leaf General Store and Diner. The store's sign was shaped like a giant maple leaf, and the front window proudly displayed shelves full of colorful plastic Bamboozlers under a banner announcing the toy's famous slogan: UNLOCK THE FUN AND FIND THE TREASURE.

"How are you, sweetie?" Mrs. Dupree asked, pulling me into a hug, her cloud of white hair brushing my cheek. A tiny bell jangled as we stepped inside the Maple Leaf. There were no customers, but the smell of hamburgers and fresh apple pie greeted us. My heart lurched when I spotted the large, unsold stack of last Friday's *Elmwood Tribune* sitting beside the still-full rack of this week's edition in the wire rack by the door.

Of course, Sauce didn't care about unsold newspapers. He bumped past my legs and charged toward the kitchen, where he knew he'd get a hamburger from Leroy, the Maple Leaf's cook, who also happens to be Mrs. Dupree's forty-something-year-old son.

"What brings you into town?" Mrs. Dupree asked. "Hunting for another scoop?"

An image of the well-dressed stranger flashed through my mind, but I shook it away. "Actually," I said, "Mom sent me to see you. She said you had payment for last month's *Tribune*?"

A bit of the usual sparkle dropped from Mrs. Dupree's brown eyes. "Of course." She walked to the store's old-fashioned cash register and clacked a few keys. The drawer dinged open, and Mrs. Dupree pulled out a white envelope. As she handed it to me, she plucked a dishrag from her apron pocket and rubbed at an invisible speck of dust on the glistening countertop. "The thing is . . ." Mrs. Dupree's voice trailed off. She kept polishing her spotless counter.

I laid my hand gently on Mrs. Dupree's. Her polishing slowed, then stopped. "Mrs. Dupree?" I said. "Is everything okay?"

"I'm sorry. It's just . . ." Mrs. Dupree's eyes lifted slowly, sadly, from their focus on the countertop. "Well, I've got to cancel my weekly order of the paper."

I stumbled back a step. "What?"

Mrs. Dupree fumbled with her dishrag, then waved it toward the stack of old *Tribune*s by the door. "Folks aren't buying papers much these days," she said. "They have their cable news channels, their computers, their phones. Pretty easy to hear what they want to hear and skip paying for articles that might make them think."

My insides twisted.

"I'm awful sorry, sweetie," Mrs. Dupree added softly. "Tell your mother that, please. . . ."

My eyes stung. "Okay, Mrs. Dupree. I will. And . . ." I swallowed back the lump in my throat. "And thank you for the payment."

By the time I coaxed Sauce from the Maple Leaf's kitchen and got him outside, I'd decided I couldn't handle telling Mom about the canceled order yet. I sent her a text:

> Got money from Mrs. D. See you at home after town meeting. Hope you get a scoop!

Mom's reply came back a minute later—a thumbs-up with a smiley emoji.

Sauce and I returned to Van Houten Park to pass the

time until we needed to meet the GEEKs at the Lookout. My bike still leaned against the base of Maxine's statue, and I slid to the ground, pressing my back against the statue's stone pedestal. Sauce snuffled my arm with his wet nose, then lay down with his head in my lap. His ears flopped across my legs like miniature blankets. It wasn't long before he was snoring.

I opened my journal to write more observations and cogitations, but I couldn't concentrate. Instead I kept looking over at the Bamboozlers in the Maple Leaf's front window. I'm sure you already know what a Bamboozler looks like—a volleyball-sized sphere of tightly packed, brightly colored rods sticking out from a central ball. The rods twist and turn and hinge, and if everything is done in just the right order, a golden button is revealed and—*sproing!*—each unique Bamboozler pops open, revealing a prize hidden at the center.

The world loved Maxine for the Bamboozler and all the other toys she invented. But Elmwood had loved her for different reasons. She had gifted the town the nature preserve and even an amusement park called Bamboozleland. She'd employed half of Elmwood at the Van Houten Toy & Game Company, giving fair pay and good benefits.

But then Maxine died and her children took over. They didn't know the first thing about running the company, unless you counted running it into the ground.

They made a series of bad decisions, starting with firing the best toy designers just to save a few bucks. Top executives and marketing people were soon fired or quit on their own because they didn't want to work with Maxine's kids. Stock prices dropped, and in an act of desperation, her son sold the Bamboozler to another toy company. The kids split the money and left town—except Alice.

All those executive offices were abandoned, and all that remained of the business was the factory. Kevin's dad and Elena's mom both still worked there, overseeing Bamboozlers being put together. But the factory had been doing less and less business since the new company started producing them elsewhere.

Elmwood began to cave in on itself, rotting away like a hollow tree. There was no golden button to be pressed. No prize at its center. Maxine had left my town with nothing but an empty promise.

My gaze slid from the theater to the hills behind it. Perched on the tallest of the hills was Van Houten Manor, silhouetted by the setting sun, looming over the town like a giant, dark tombstone.

Except that it *wasn't* totally dark. A single light glowed from its highest window. I sat up. Sauce lifted his head from my lap. His tail began to thump against the grass.

FACT #1: Alice Van Houten is dead.

FACT #2: So is every other Van Houten who ever lived in the manor.

FACT #3: Ghosts are not real.

So who just turned on the light?
I shifted my legs, ready to investigate.
BONG! . . .
The church's bell tower began to toll the hour.
BONG! . . .
The Lookout! I leapt to my feet. Sauce scrambled up with me. I was supposed to meet the GEEKs. And despite Kevin's complaints about missing the town meeting, he'd chow all the taquitos and cookies if he got the chance.

Sauce and I took off—me pedaling like crazy, him enjoying a rare ride in my bike's basket. Sauce gave a happy howl, his long ears flapping behind him, two streamers in the wind. I could hardly wait to tell the GEEKs about the stranger I'd spotted and about the light at Van Houten Manor!

We flew up Sap Run Road, bumped across the empty field behind Elmwood Middle School, and skidded to a stop by the fence that separated the field from the nature preserve. As I dropped my bike to the ground,

Sauce wriggled through our secret, hidden gap in the fence. I peeled the fence back a little further to squeeze through after him, tugging at his leash to slow him.

Long before I was born, the preserve included well-groomed paths dotted with signs highlighting the wide variety of native plants and animals. Now, although the preserve's trees still pointed majestically toward the sky, its trails were a tangle of undergrowth speckled with half-rotted signposts. I followed the sounds of snapping twigs and rustling underbrush, struggling to keep up with Sauce as I navigated the shadowy woods with the reading light I always kept clipped to my notebook.

"About time, Gee!" Elena called, peering over the railing as Sauce and I reached the Lookout.

"There better still be some food," I said, scooping Sauce up and climbing the ladder. There was just enough moonlight to help me skip the broken rungs and avoid the slippery patches of moss.

The Lookout was basically a square porch on really tall stilts. It had a three-foot-high railing, though half the rails were rotten and splintered. The only gap in the railing was for the ladder. A giant hole in the roof let water in during rainstorms, but otherwise, it was the perfect secret hangout.

We kept the DANGER: CONDEMNED sign in place to discourage trespassers.

As we crunched on spicy, still-warm taquitos, Kevin knocked twice on the floor of the Lookout. "I officially call this meeting of the GEEKs to order!"

"And I officially declare that no more official calls to order are allowed," Elena said.

"You can't do that," Kevin said. "I'm trying to prepare for my class presidency. You already forced me to skip the town meeting. The least you can do is let me establish formal, democratic protocols for the GEEKs."

The rest of us shared an eye roll. Except for Sauce. He was busy licking deep-fried-taquito crumbs from the container while Edgar scratched between his ears.

"We all want you to get elected," I said, helping myself to the biggest cookie, "but can't we talk about something else first? I was in the park this afternoon and—"

"Gina, you're the one who said I can't let Sophina bully me," Kevin said. "And you're right. I can't drop out of the race just because she's popular."

"Exactly," I said. "But listen, when I was at the park—"

"We all love Elmwood, but it's seen better days, the school included. And if I win, I think I could finally make a real difference." Kevin bounced excitedly as he spoke. "Finally turn things around. *That's* what this campaign should be about!"

I gave up on trying to tell the GEEKs about the man I'd seen walk out of Thomas Ridley's law office that afternoon. Or about the strange light I'd noticed at Van

Houten Manor. As Kevin rambled on about his election campaign, I gazed from the Lookout, half listening, half daydreaming. I stared down at the overgrown forest, the spire of the church peeking out above the trees, and beyond that the abandoned rides of Bamboozleland.

That's when I glimpsed it. A flashlight beam brought my focus back to the forest below. A shadowy shape. It slid along an overgrown path, heading toward the edge of the preserve, moving toward Van Houten Manor.

"Hey," I whispered. "Look! I saw something." I pointed toward the path winding between the trees. "A person."

"You sure, Gee?" Elena asked, squinting toward the trail. "No one else is ever in the preserve."

"Probably just a deer," Edgar added.

"No," I said. "I know what I saw." I looked, hoping for another glimpse, wishing for more than a flash of light and a moonlit shadow. But there was nothing. Still, it wasn't my imagination. Somewhere down below us, someone was moving through the preserve. And my reporter radar told me one thing—that *someone* was a slight man in a charcoal-gray suit.

Friday, September 17

Observations & COGITATIONS

(Van Houten Park)

— Elmwood Community Church choir practicing "Amazing Grace"; tenors are flat

— Ms. Lavoie snipped rose from town square flower garden

⤳ IS IT STEALING OR ARE THE ROSES PUBLIC PROPERTY?

— Fire Chief Ambrose Pringle sitting outside Elmwood FD, tilting back on two legs of plastic chair

⤳ SHOULDN'T A FIRE CHIEF MODEL SAFER BEHAVIOR?

— Katy Phelps & Brandon Carwinkle digging for worms by maple tree; Mrs. Phelps & Mrs. Carwinkle sitting 20 feet away, talking, barely paying attention to kids

⤳ WHAT ARE THEY GOING TO DO WITH ALL THE WORMS?

— Unknown man visited Thomas Ridley's law office: slight; slicked-back brown hair (thinning); charcoal-gray suit; blue tie; black leather shoes (polished); large yellow envelope & ring of keys

⤳ WHO IS HE?

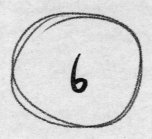

"Come on," I whispered, picking up Sauce and heading for the ladder. "We have to follow him."

"We can't stalk a stranger through the woods at night!" Kevin said.

"And how do you know it's a *him*?" Edgar asked.

"I'll explain as we go." I eased my way down the ladder—not an easy task while cradling Sauce in one arm. "Just stay quiet."

To the rest of the GEEKs' credit, they all kept quiet and followed me from the Lookout. When I got to the ground, I kept Sauce in my arms so he couldn't run off.

"Okay, Gee, what's this all about?" Elena whispered.

I started leading them toward the trail. "We have to go to Van Houten Manor."

Kevin halted, grabbing my arm. "Are you nuts? That place is off-limits!"

"Technically, Kev, so is the Lookout," Elena said. "Let Gee talk."

"Here's the deal," I said. "Before I came to the Lookout, I was in the park and saw a light go on in Van Houten Manor." In the shadowy moonlight, I could see all the others turn toward me. I definitely had their attention now. "And that's not the only odd thing I've seen today. . . ."

The others listened as we crept along the trail and I explained about the stranger leaving Thomas Ridley's law office and heading toward Scrubstone Lane. How I was sure I'd just now spotted the same stranger slipping through the woods. How I thought he might be the person snooping around in Van Houten Manor.

"But who is he?" Elena asked.

"I don't know," I said. "But I have a guess." I smiled, unable to resist keeping at least a *little* mystery alive.

And if I'm right, I thought, *it may be a much bigger scoop than whatever's going on at the town meeting.*

About ten minutes later, we stepped from the preserve and onto the edge of the Van Houten estate. Our footsteps crunched on the gravel driveway as we approached the house, which leaned forward like it was preparing to dive down the hillside. It was the closest I'd ever been to the sprawling three-story mansion. After all, up until a month ago it had been protected by a ninety-four-year-old woman armed with a paintball bazooka.

Even in the dim light, I could make out the peeling clapboard and the broken railing of the wraparound porch. A crumbling stone chimney climbed the house, and half the windows were boarded over. The shutters that hadn't already dropped to the ground clung cock-eyed on single hinges, and the roof was a hodgepodge of peaks and valleys, angles and lines. A turret stuck up from the middle of the house, rising above the third story. A single light glowed from the turret's highest window like the beacon from a lighthouse.

Sauce was still in my arms. But my arms were beginning to ache. He may not be a big dog, but he's a chubby one. I set him on the ground. "No more taking off," I muttered as Edgar knelt to pet him.

Sauce looked up at me, eyes all wide and innocent. Not buying his act even a little, I tied his leash to the most secure porch railing I could see.

"Now what?" Kevin asked, his voice shaking slightly.

"Duh," Elena said. "Isn't it obvious?" She marched

onto the porch and pounded on the front door. "Hello?" she called. "Anyone home?"

No footsteps. No new lights. Nothing.

"We should go back," Kevin said. "No one's here."

"Not yet," I replied. I stepped up to the door and knocked again. "Give him time to open the door."

"What are you so scared of?" Elena asked. "There's four of us and only one of him."

"I'm not scared," Kevin said. "I'm just . . . cautious."

Elena snorted.

Behind me, Sauce whined. He looked at me, then cocked his head to one side. "What is it, boy?" I asked. "Is something—"

"Rah-oo!" Sauce took off, tugging the porch post down. The broken post banged along after him for a couple of beats before his leash slipped free. Then he skittered around the corner of the porch and out of sight.

"Sauce!" I gave chase, rounding one corner of the porch, then another. "Not *again!*"

The others followed me, their footsteps pounding. I got to the back of the house just in time to see Sauce squeeze his long, chubby body through a tiny door labeled OTIS.

I dove for Sauce's tail, only to come up with air and belly-flop onto the porch.

I lurched to my knees and shoved my head through the cat door. Too dark. When I pulled my head back out, Elena, Edgar, and Kevin stood huddled behind me.

"I *told* you guys we should have gone back," Kevin said.

"Drop it," I snapped. "Right now, the only thing that matters is getting Sauce."

"What we need to get," Kevin said, "is *help.*"

Elena popped her knuckles. "We can handle this. All we need is a little nitric acid. If we drip it into the locking mechanism, the chemical reaction should—"

"No way!" Kevin protested. "We can't go around breaking and entering!"

"Um . . . guys?" Edgar said.

"We won't *be* breaking and entering," Elena said. "We'll just be melting a lock, opening a door, and maybe going inside for a little bit. It's an emergency, Kev! We gotta get to Sauce!"

"Guys?" Edgar said again.

"I'm running for class president," Kevin argued. "I can't be—"

Crack! Edgar stomped his foot so hard the entire porch shook. *"Guys!"*

Kevin and Elena stared at Edgar. So did I. The only time I'd ever heard Edgar yell was when he'd played a drill sergeant in the fifth-grade play.

"Why don't we just try the door?" Then he turned the doorknob.

The door creaked inward on rusty hinges. I almost laughed with relief.

"See?" Elena told Kevin. "No one's breaking. Only entering."

Kevin swallowed his protest and followed the rest of us into the kitchen of Van Houten Manor. Edgar had started humming "The Room Where It Happens" under his breath.

The first thing I did was flick the light switch. Nothing. Apparently, the power had been cut after Alice Van Houten died, which made me wonder about the light in the turret. All four of us shone our cell phones around the large kitchen. Cupboards hung open. Dishes, pots, and pans littered the counters. Boards had been torn from the floor, holes punched in walls. The kitchen smelled like a mixture of sour milk, mildew, and old cat.

"Sauce?" I called. The floorboards creaked as I stepped over an old spaghetti strainer. "Sauce?" I held my breath.

"Rah-oooooo . . ." came a muffled, distant howl.

I sprang into the next room—a dining room. The others trailed behind me. No Sauce. We dodged around a broken chair and a tipped-over china cabinet, weaving from room to room, following the narrow lights of our phones. A living room. A second dining room. A library. More messes, more destruction, no Sauce.

"Rah-oooooo . . ."

"Sauce!" we all yelled, trying to figure out where his howl was coming from.

"Rah-oooooo . . ."

Then we found stairs. Faint light spilled from high above. This time, when Sauce howled, there was no doubt where the sound was coming from. We charged up one flight of stairs. A second. Sauce's howls drew closer. So did the light.

Finally, at the top of the turret, we stumbled into some sort of office. A battery-operated lantern sat on a scuffed, dust-covered oak desk beneath the room's only window. Bookshelves lined two of the four walls, although all the books lay strewn across the floor, half their pages missing. Two red velvet chairs and a small couch had their cushions slashed, tufts of white stuffing sticking out. And there was Sauce, his nose in the air, howling at a tattered, floor-to-ceiling tapestry of an old guy with a long, white beard and a floppy, goofy-looking hat. Thanks to Mr. Singh's social studies class, I knew the tapestry pictured the famous artist and inventor Leonardo da Vinci.

"Sauce!" I dropped to my knees and wrapped my dog in a hug. He slurped his tongue across my cheek. "You have to stop running off like that!"

"Okay," Kevin said. "We found him. Let's go before we get caught."

But before we could go anywhere, Sauce wriggled from my arms and started howling at the tapestry again.

"That's weird," I said. "He doesn't usually howl at art."

Edgar pursed his lips. "Everyone's a critic."

"Wait." Elena cupped a hand to her ear. "Do you hear that?"

Sauce's howls paused just long enough for me to make out a faint *thump-thump* that sounded like Leonardo da Vinci was trying to escape his own portrait. I leapt to my feet and hauled the tapestry aside. Hidden behind it was a massive steel door with a large digital keypad lock.

Thump-thump-thump.

"Someone's trapped in there!" I tugged on the door. It didn't budge. "It's probably the man I was telling you about!"

Edgar cupped his hands around his mouth right by the door and shouted, "Don't worry! We're here!"

Kevin put his mouth to the door too. "What's the combination?" he called.

The only response was more thumping and some muffled, indecipherable shouts. Still, we didn't give up. Edgar and Kevin kept shouting. Sauce kept howling. I kept tugging. But it was Elena who took *real* action.

"Wait here," she said. "I'll be right back." Elena dashed from the room and hurtled down the stairs. A minute later she returned, breathing hard, holding a small, pale-yellow box.

"What's that?" Edgar asked.

"Cornstarch," Elena replied. "From the kitchen. Expired twenty years ago, but that won't matter." Elena tore off the top of the box, grabbed a fistful of her own dark hair, and dipped the tips into the cornstarch.

Kevin's forehead wrinkled. "What are you doing?"

"Obviously, I'd rather use a paintbrush," Elena said, swiping the powdery tips of her hair over the steel door's digital lock, "but I didn't have time to find one."

"But—"

"Plus, we're in a hurry. Who knows how much oxygen is left in there?"

"But—"

"Watch and learn," Elena said. She turned toward me. "Hey, Gee, shine your phone on the lock."

I did as she ordered and watched as faint, powdery fingerprints appeared on four keys of the digital keypad.

"One, two, seven, and nine," Elena said, reading the four numbers aloud.

"Okay, that was pretty cool," Kevin admitted. "But we still don't know the order. Those four digits could be randomly sequenced in twenty-four possible combinations, but—"

"A four-digit code?" Elena interrupted. "You think whoever put this giant steel door here is only going to protect whatever's behind it with a *four*-digit code?"

Kevin grit his teeth. "If you had let me *finish*," he said, "I was just about to say that it's more likely that a six-digit code has been used for extra security, so at least one of the four digits had to be used more than once. The number of random combinations would actually be—"

"Somebody might have made up the combination they wanted," I said. "Something they could remember. What if it wasn't random?"

Kevin scratched his head. "Six digits . . . I suppose it could be a date."

The thumping and muffled shouts from the other side of the door continued, a constant reminder that we needed to hurry.

"The seven is more faded than the others," I said. "Actually, a lot more faded. It must be one that repeats."

"Gina's right," Edgar said.

"Just . . ." Kevin took a few ragged breaths through clenched teeth. "Just give me a second to think." He scrubbed his hands over his eyes. "A seven could mean a July date, but if it's been used more than once, there would need to be a seven in the year—"

"Or it could be the seventh of July," Elena said.

The thumping grew faster, more frantic.

Maxine had probably programmed the code, so it would have been a number or date that was meaningful to her. My eyes lingered on the *seven* and the *nine*. *Seventy-nine*. Why was that number familiar?

"Could it be a date from 1979?" I asked, thinking aloud.

"Or the 1790s!" Edgar cried. "Maybe it's a date from the French Revolution. Raise a glass to freedom!"

He sang this last part. *Hamilton* again. Mid-eye roll, an image snapped into my mind. The engraving above the doorway of town hall . . .

Elena turned to give Edgar a blank stare. "And does the French Revolution have anything to do with Van Houten Manor, or just your *Hamilton* obsession?"

"No, Edgar's right!" I said. "Well, about the 1700s, at least." I turned to Elena. "Try seven-two-one-seven-seven-nine—July second, 1779—the founding date of Elmwood!"

Elena punched in the code. A green light flashed at the top of the keypad. There was a soft click.

Lots of times, a reporter has to take the facts and then trust her gut. My hunch had been right about unlocking the door. It had *also* been right about who'd been trapped behind it.

A man—*the* man—stumbled from an empty vault, gasping for air. His gray suit was rumpled, his blue tie loosened around his neck. He wasn't very tall—Edgar had him by a couple of inches. His thinning brown hair, which had been slicked back the first time I'd seen him, was now spiked in all directions and damp with sweat. A stubbly beard shadowed his face. "She booby-trapped the vault door," he mumbled to himself, his blue eyes wide. Then he blinked, focusing on us for the first time. "You—you saved me. But how did you know I was here?"

"My dog found you." I pointed at Sauce. "We were just chasing after him. Then we heard the pounding." I studied the man, comparing him to the statue of Maxine Van Houten in the park. They didn't look much alike, but they both had long noses and similar shoulders, and here he was in Van Houten Manor. I had to know if my hunch was correct. "Are you Maxwell Van Houten?"

I held my breath. If I was right, then this man was Alice Van Houten's nephew and the only surviving descendant of Maxine Van Houten.

My question seemed to snap him from his daze. "I'm sorry," he said. "Where are my manners? Yes, of course I am." He reached out to shake my hand. "But please— call me Max. And thank you for saving me from her— from Aunt Alice's trap."

My heartbeat quickened with excitement. *I was right!*

Max smiled, his eyes crinkling at the edges while he smoothed out the wrinkles in his suit. "It sure didn't take you long to figure out who I was. Let me guess—

you also must have been the one who figured out the combination."

Heat rushed to my face at the man's—Max's—compliment. "Well . . ."

"It was a team effort," Kevin said. "We *all* figured it out."

"Ah, of course," Max said, but I thought I detected a knowing twinkle in his eyes. Then he sank into a wobbly chair behind the oak desk. "I hope you don't mind if I sit down. Please, join me."

Sauce had apparently been waiting for an invitation. He leapt onto the torn-up couch, sending a cloud of dust puffing into the air. Elena and I sat down beside him. Kevin and Edgar each sat in one of the ragged red-velvet chairs.

As soon as we'd all introduced ourselves (and Sauce, of course), Max leaned his elbows on the desk and rested his chin in his hands. "So, Gina, you said Sauce sniffed me out. But what brought you up to the manor in the first place?"

I thought of Elmwood's run-down park. All the houses for sale. The newspaper's lost subscribers. I tried to keep the hope from my voice as I asked, "Are you . . . are you here to help the town?" Even though I deal in facts, not luck, I crossed my fingers.

"Help?" Max asked. "How?"

"I saw you leaving Thomas Ridley's law office this

afternoon. I thought you must have some money left from your grandma's company." I shoved down the memory of the FINAL NOTICE paper on my mom's desk. "I thought maybe you'd use it to help Elmwood, like she always said she would."

Max rubbed at the shadow of beard on his cheeks for a long moment. "Let me be honest with you," he said. "I'm not proud of the way my family acted after my grandmother's death. I was sent off to boarding school at Grantwood Prep from the age of twelve, so I missed most of it. But it didn't take them long to drive the company into the ground, then squander what little profits remained on vacation homes and expensive parties, instead of reinvesting in the company." Max looked slowly from me, to Elena, to Edgar, to Kevin. "In short, I'm as broke as Elmwood."

So this is what having your hopes dashed feels like, I thought.

"Aunt Alice's lawyer—Mr. Ridley—shared another bit of unexpected news with me today, as well," Max continued. "Your mayor just finished sharing it with the rest of the town."

The town meeting, I thought.

The GEEKs all looked at Max. I held my breath.

"Apparently," Max said, "when my uncle sold the Bamboozler to a rival toy company, their agreement stated that the Elmwood factory would only be able to continue producing Bamboozlers for a certain amount of time. That time is now up."

Edgar blinked. "What's that mean?"

Kevin's eyes were wide. "It means the Van Houten Toy and Game Company will be shutting down for good." He swallowed and glanced at Elena. "Which means my dad and Elena's mom won't have jobs anymore."

Elena looked like she might be sick. "They can't do that! The people here have dedicated their lives to making Bamboozlers. They belong to Elmwood!" I put a hand on Elena's arm, but she shrugged it off. She glared at Max. "My mom has worked at Van Houten Toys for twenty years!"

Max raised his hands in surrender. "I'm sorry," he said. "Truly. I didn't know anything about this until today. It's out of my control."

Elena rolled her eyes. Sauce — smart, sensitive Sauce — nuzzled her arm, then laid his head in her lap.

The toy company shutting down forever? This wasn't the scoop I'd been hoping for when we'd followed the trail to Van Houten Manor. It might be the factory closing, but it wasn't just the factory jobs at stake. Who would be left in town to afford a newspaper? What would Mom and I do?

I blinked back tears, wishing I could bury my face in Sauce's fur.

For a long time, no one spoke; no one moved.

Then Max cleared his throat. He nodded to himself like he'd made a decision. "I don't have any money to help Elmwood. And I can't get the Bamboozler back. But . . . well, maybe *together* we can do something."

Kevin sat forward on his chair. "What do you mean?"

"I assume you've heard the stories about my grandmother?" Max asked. "About how she supposedly gambled away her entire fortune?"

"Of course," we all said.

"The thing is," Max replied slowly, "I always believed those stories. I thought squandering money must simply run in the family. But when I arrived at the manor earlier today, I found something interesting." He pulled open a drawer on the desk and drew out a couple of sheets of yellowed paper filled with old-fashioned typewriter lettering. He handed them to me. "Go ahead, Gina. Read them out loud. I think you'll agree"—Max's blue eyes sparkled as they met mine—"those two sheets of paper could change *everything.*"

April 2, 1987

Greetings, fellow citizens of Elmwood. Thank you for joining me this evening. I realize I've been rather cryptic regarding the purpose of this town meeting, so I appreciate your willingness to indulge my eccentricities. After a lifetime of puzzle making, I suppose such secrecy is a habit I'm incapable of breaking.

I requested today's gathering for two reasons. I have both good news and bad news. However, I have never been a person who dwells on the negative, so I will dispense with the bad news first and state it plainly: I am very sick.

In recent months, I have taken numerous trips to New York City to consult with medical specialists. The news has not been good, and the time I have left is short. However, I will not linger on this fact. Instead, I must ask you all to accept one simple truth: We must go on, because we can't turn back.

Now, on to the good news. You may have heard whispers about my intentions, and the whispers are true: I will leave my fortune to this town. However, the years have forced me to accept the ill effects greed can have on people. Therefore, I want to ensure that my fortune will be managed by a worthy steward. I have thought at length of how this might be achieved. Ultimately, I determined to take the route most consistent with my life's work. I made one last puzzle.

My fortune is now hidden within the town of Elmwood—a town I have loved so dearly— along a path that can only be uncovered by a worthy seeker who is able to untangle the clues and interpret the signs. For as long as the finder of my fortune lives, he or she will be entrusted to use that fortune solely for the service of this great town.

Here is the first clue:

8

I hadn't even looked up from reading the letter's last line before Elena—who was reading over my shoulder—blurted, "Wait! What? That's it? Mad Maxine wrote, 'Here is the first clue,' then *stopped*? Oh, sweet Einstein, you've *got* to be kidding me!" She snatched the two pages from my hands and flipped them over.

Something about Maxine's words sounded familiar, but I couldn't figure out why.

"I found the letter in here," Max said. He tapped the top of the desk. "Look at the date—April second, 1987. Maxine—my grandmother—died the very next day. That means she never got to call the town meeting. She never got to give this speech."

I suddenly thought of the rumors about Maxine's mysterious trips from town and how she'd been blowing her fortune on bingo. In reality, she'd been visiting doctors in New York. Even I had believed those rumors. Instead I should have been looking for facts.

"So we've been wrong about Maxine all this time," I murmured. "Maybe she gave the letter to Alice so she could deliver the message for her, or maybe Alice just found it after Maxine died. Either way, it's not *Maxine's* fault Alice kept the information secret. Plus, it explains all of *this*." I kicked at a loose floorboard and grabbed a wad of stuffing from one of the slashed couch cushions. "Alice had been searching for the fortune since 1987."

"It also explains the booby-trapped vault door," Edgar said.

"And don't forget Alice's paintball bazooka!" Elena added.

"The thing is," Kevin said, "now that we know all of this, we can't keep it a secret. My mom's on the select board. Elena's dad is chief of police. We've got to tell them about this. They'll know what to do." Kevin stood and took a step toward the door.

"Wait," Max said, a new firmness in his voice.

Kevin froze, physically incapable of disobeying a direct adult order.

"I was at tonight's meeting," Max said, his voice softening. "I'd planned to read my grandmother's farewell address to everyone. But . . . well, when people heard the news about the Bamboozler, they were surprised, worried, angry. They started shouting and arguing over who to blame and what to do. Suddenly, I had second thoughts about reading the letter." He sighed. "I'm afraid the search for the fortune would tear the town apart, not bring it together."

I wanted to defend my town. But what if Max was right? "You make it sound as if the people at the meeting acted more like enemies than neighbors," I said.

Max nodded. "That's a rather apt description."

"How do we know you don't just want to find the fortune for yourself, like Alice?" Kevin asked.

Max's eyes widened slightly. He seemed stung by this remark. "If we find the fortune, I have every intention of abiding by my grandmother's wishes," he said. "The money will belong to Elmwood. But it's like she said in her speech. We need a worthy seeker to find the fortune. Or, perhaps . . ." Max looked each of us in the eye. "*Four* worthy seekers."

Sauce barked.

Max laughed. "My apologies, Sauce. *Five*."

"You mean . . . us?" I said, my voice barely a whisper.

"By saving me from the vault, you proved you have exceptional problem-solving skills." Max looked right at Kevin. "All *four* of you proved that."

Kevin stood a little straighter.

"And Gina's first question for me was whether I was here to help the town," Max added. "While everyone else is probably still arguing, you've shown me how much you care about Elmwood. I can't think of anyone better suited to undertake this quest. To solve my grandmother's final puzzle."

"But how can we do that?" Elena asked. "We don't have the first clue."

Max pulled out one final sheet of paper. His eyes twinkled. "Oh yes," he said, "we do."

Life's not a matter of holding good cards,

but of playing a poor hand well.

If you're seeking out a Scholar's treasure,

then look To his citadel.

There in the highest pinnacle

of our humble little town,

your Eye will glimpse the sour key

that leads you to my crown.

If you've ever learned about a hidden treasure that
could save your town, then you probably understand
why I was anxious for the GEEKs to solve the clue.
You also probably understand why I didn't get much
sleep Friday night and why I wasn't too excited about
spending my entire Saturday morning at the Elmwood
Farmers Market.

But the farmers market took place in the town park
every Saturday, rain or shine (and sometimes snow),
from eight in the morning until noon. And every Saturday, Edgar was required to be there at the Feingarten
Family Farms stall, selling things like fresh milk, butter,
and cheese.

So that's where the rest of us had to be, too. Elena
was helping Edgar at his stall. I'd agreed to help Kevin,

who had decided that the farmers market was the perfect place to advertise his election campaign.

Apparently, campaigns never stop. Even for treasure.

As Sauce and I headed toward the table Kevin had set up near the gazebo, I couldn't help but notice the sparse crowd. The farmers market used to be bursting with stalls, as townspeople and visitors packed into Elmwood for farm-fresh produce, handcrafted jewelry, maple syrup, and more. Now there were only a handful of stalls sprinkled around the park. A few shoppers wandered aimlessly from stall to stall, but hardly any of them bothered to buy anything. Most still looked sad or upset (or both) from the previous night's town meeting, which my mom confirmed had involved a bunch of townspeople shouting and arguing, just like Max had said.

The only person who seemed to be enjoying herself was Sophina Burkhart.

Sauce almost tripped over his own tongue as we passed the Burkhart Bakery booth, which filled the air with the smell of fresh breads, muffins, and doughnuts. But I had learned my lesson yesterday. Today I had his leash wound three times around my hand.

Sophina sat in front of the booth on a high-backed stool, talking loudly to two sixth-grade admirers, smirking toward Kevin's table the entire time. "When you vote for me," she said, her voice carrying across the nearly empty market, "you're voting to make Elmwood Middle the best, funnest school in New Hampshire!"

"*Funnest* isn't even a word," I mumbled to myself, scowling toward Sophina as I hurried past. I should have been less concerned about grammar and more concerned about watching where I was going.

"*Oof!*" I grunted, knocking into someone.

"Oh my!" cried a stooped woman whose straight, white hair hung down the back of her burgundy dress. She was even shorter than me and thin as a tightly rolled newspaper. Her voice had a slight accent I couldn't place, but I knew she lived in Elmwood. I'd seen her around town, though I didn't know her name. I managed to catch her just as she was about to topple over.

"I'm sorry!" I said, holding her upright. "I was—"

"Don't worry, dear," the woman said, the *r*'s of *worry* and *dear* rolling softly on her tongue. "You simply caught me by surprise." The woman straightened the thick, round-framed glasses perched on the end of her beaklike nose. She patted my arm. "I'm right as rain."

I took another moment to make sure she really was okay before Sauce and I hustled over to Kevin.

Kevin had taped a sheet of yellow construction paper to the edge of his table:

KEVIN ROBINSON FOR
6TH-GRADE CLASS PRESIDENT
Elmwood Middle School

"Veteran leadership. Fresh ideas.
A brand-new start."

Unfortunately, Kevin had tried to fit too much onto the paper, so he'd had to write kind of small. You couldn't read it unless you stood less than ten feet away. In the middle of the table sat a three-inch-thick stack of election flyers held down by a Fighting Sap Tappers paperweight. (Yes, the Fighting Sap Tappers. Don't mock our school mascot.)

"No one's come to my table, Gina," Kevin said. "*No one.*"

"Be patient. I'm sure someone will stop by."

Kevin grunted and gazed gloomily off toward Sophina, who'd been joined by three more middle schoolers. She handed them doughnuts from a box on her lap, and Kevin's shoulders drooped.

"At least once the market's over, we can work on the clue," I said.

His head whipped toward me. "You took the clue last night. Haven't you already made progress?"

I tried to ignore the annoyance in Kevin's voice. I knew he was under serious campaign pressure. I kept my voice calm and said, "No, no progress yet. I figured all the GEEKs could work on it together."

In truth, I had been thinking about the clue all night. I just hadn't been able to crack it. The worst part was, there was something staring me right in the face. I could feel it—I just couldn't see it.

"Well, I noticed last night that *Scholar's, To,* and *Eye* were capitalized," Kevin said. "Those words are obviously important."

"Yeah," I said, starting to get annoyed myself now. "I saw that too. Maybe we should go check in with Edgar and Elena and see what they think."

Kevin pointed to his flyers. "You want me to abandon my table? What if someone wants details on my school-improvement plan?"

I raised an eyebrow and slowly turned my head from side to side. No one was even sneezing toward Kevin's table, let alone requesting details about his election campaign.

Kevin took my hint. "Fine," he mumbled. He straightened his stack of flyers, and we headed toward the stall for Feingarten Family Farms.

As soon as we walked up, Edgar moaned, "One pint

71

of milk and a pound of butter." He looked as bummed as Kevin. "The market's been open for an hour and a half, and that's all we've sold—a single jug of milk and some stinking butter."

"I've told Edge he needs to dress in a cow costume," Elena said. "I'm sure bovine acting skills will be in high demand someday, plus it would totally attract more customers."

I cringed. Edgar didn't talk about it much, but I knew he worried about the farm. His parents sold milk and other products to local restaurants and schools and even to the toy factory's cafeteria. If the factory and other businesses closed, the whole farm—including Edgar's prizewinning heifer, Ollie—might have to be sold.

If the town of Elmwood collapsed, we *all* had a lot to lose.

I was about to ask Edgar and Elena if they had any thoughts about the clue when someone behind us exclaimed, "I can't believe that man has the audacity to show his face around town!"

I turned. It was Sophina's mom, who had wandered over from the bakery booth to chat with Mrs. Feingarten. Mrs. Burkhart had the same blond hair as Sophina, though hers was pulled back in a ponytail so tight I was surprised she could still scowl. When I followed the path of her death stare, I spotted Max Van Houten standing by the gazebo. His suit had been replaced by navy blue slacks and a crisp, white dress shirt, open at the collar.

Mrs. Burkhart planted her hands on her hips. "I heard from Charlene who heard from Ethel who has it on good authority from Tom Ridley's housekeeper that that man is Maxwell Van Houten himself. Does he think he's going to come in here and strip away what little this town has left?"

"Now, Melinda," Mrs. Feingarten said reasonably, "let's give the poor man a chance. He just lost his aunt. He's in mourning. And sorting out the Van Houten estate must feel overwhelming."

"*Hmph,*" Mrs. Burkhart grunted.

Apparently, Mrs. Burkhart wasn't the only one who had heard about Max's arrival. And she wasn't the only one upset with him either.

Elena gripped my arm as Mr. Herman, who worked in the toy factory and ran a stall selling hand-carved garden sculptures, stalked up to Max and started shouting. "I know who you are, and you're not welcome here!"

His finger was pointed right in Max's face.

Max took a step back. "I'm sorry. I—"

"If your grandmother had kept her word—or if your uncle and his ilk hadn't sold off the prize jewel of the company—Elmwood would be in fine condition. We wouldn't be stuck with *this*!" Mr. Herman swept his arms wide, indicating the nearly empty farmers market.

Mabel Picard—from the Mabel's Maple Syrup stall—joined the confrontation: "We know you're still hiding some of that fortune. You *have* to be." She wagged a finger in Max's face, backing him up against the broken latticework of the gazebo. "The least you can do is help the town that made your family so rich!"

I was beginning to understand why Max had decided not to read Maxine's letter at the town meeting. He was right. I'd never seen this sort of anger in Elmwood before. Even in the half-deserted farmers market, the people seemed more like an angry mob and less like the neighbors I passed on my way to school every day. The neighbors who brought soup to sick neighbors and shoveled snow from each other's driveways. What was happening to us?

The other GEEKs and I locked eyes. In unspoken agreement, we eased our way toward the gazebo. We had to keep our secret—we couldn't explain to the townsfolk that Max actually *was* trying to help the town. But at least we could be close by if he needed help.

"Look," Max said kindly to Mr. Herman and Ms. Picard, "I wish I had a fortune. But I don't. I'm only here to clean out Aunt Alice's house." He pulled a wallet from the back pocket of his slacks and smiled. "And of course, to support all of you fine folk at the farmers market."

Mr. Herman and Ms. Picard didn't quite smile back, but they looked considerably happier after Max bought a hand-carved garden gnome from Mr. Herman plus a few bottles of Mabel's Maple Syrup. By the time Max had visited every stall in the market, he'd even ordered five pounds of cheddar from Edgar's mom.

Before leaving, Max stopped by Kevin's table and picked up one of the flyers. "Nice," he said, nodding at Kevin. "You created a very professional layout."

Max winked at me as Kevin beamed.

"I also have something for all of you." Max set down a box of blueberry muffins from Burkhart Bakery. "Brain food for fortune hunters," he whispered.

Elena glanced at Kevin, who looked offended by the presence of anything associated with Sophina Burkhart. Then Elena picked up a muffin and crammed the whole thing into her mouth. "Sorry, Kev," she said. A half-chewed blueberry dropped from her lips and plopped onto Kevin's stack of flyers. "I know Sophina's annoying. But a girl's gotta eat."

10

Max's visit to the farmers market ended up being exactly what we needed to kick-start our treasure hunt:

FACT #1: Mrs. Feingarten was so excited about Max's five-pound order of cheddar that she told Edgar, "Honey, go enjoy the rest of the morning with your friends."

FACT #2: Kevin was so upset about the blueberry muffins that he said, "I can't compete against baked goods. Let's leave."

FACT #3: Six and a half minutes later, we were following Sauce through the gap in the fence into the nature preserve, on our way to the Lookout.

As soon as we'd climbed up, I pulled the clue from between the pages of my notebook.

Kevin grabbed it from my hand and pointed to *Scholar's, To,* and *Eye.* "See?" he said. "These are capitalized but shouldn't be."

Edgar twirled one of his loopy curls around one finger. "Maybe those words make an anagram or something."

"No problem," Elena said. "I got this." She whisper-spelled the words to herself, then started to rearrange the letters to make new words. "How about 'Lose sore yacht'?"

"Come on," Kevin said. "This isn't a joke."

"Maybe 'Cheesy solo art'!"

"Elena!"

"Let's focus on the rest of the clue," I said, jumping in. We didn't need to start fighting like the rest of the town. "What about *citadel* and *pinnacle*? A *citadel* is a fortress, like a castle, and castles were usually built on high ground. And a *pinnacle* is a high point or peak. Both words suggest somewhere high."

"The Lookout is high," Edgar said.

We all looked around our run-down hideout.

"I think we'd have noticed by now if there were a clue to buried treasure here," said Kevin.

Elena pointed north. "Van Houten Manor is even higher. It's the highest point in Elmwood."

"Alice only ever searched the manor," Kevin said. "She barely even left it." He started doing his excited bounce. "She probably knew something we don't!"

I rubbed Sauce's head. "If the next clue was there, don't you think Alice would have found it? You saw the manor. She tore it apart, room by room, for decades."

"You're probably right," Edgar said. "But we have to start somewhere. We might as well check Kevin's idea."

Kevin raised his chin, his lips curving into a smug smile.

"Fine," I said. Even though Kevin was starting to get on my nerves, I didn't want to argue. Plus, Edgar was right—we had to start somewhere.

Max opened the door as soon as we knocked. His sleeves were rolled up past his elbows, his white shirt covered in dusty smudges. He swiped the back of one hand across his sweaty forehead. "Run out of muffins?"

"You're a mess," Elena said.

Max laughed. "So is this house." He wiped his hands on his untucked shirttail and reached down to pat Sauce on the head. "Any luck with the clue?"

"Well," I said, "in the clue, the words *citadel* and—"

"*Citadel* and *pinnacle* are both words dealing with height," Kevin said, leapfrogging my explanation. "That may mean the clue is hidden somewhere high up. And Van Houten Manor is the highest point in Elmwood."

Max rubbed his chin, then shook his head. "I doubt it. Every pillow, cushion, and mattress in this house has had stuffing removed. And every wall has holes punched through it. If the fortune were here, Aunt Alice would've found it."

Kevin frowned. I barely stopped myself from giving him an *I told you so* double eyebrow raise.

Max pointed to a jumble of boxes near the door. "Just look at all the ruined books. Every one has pages torn out. That woman was thorough."

I'd noticed the torn-up books the night before, but this was the first time I'd really paid attention. It was worse than I'd thought. The boxes were filled with classics like *Alice's Adventures in Wonderland* and *Peter Pan*. I'd read all of them with Mom. Then my eyes settled on one we'd read many times—*Treasure Island*. Mom did a mean pirate voice.

And that's when something finally clicked.

"We must go on, because we can't turn back!" I blurted.

"Huh?" Kevin asked.

"We got so focused on the clue," I said, "we ignored Maxine's letter to the town." I snatched the torn-up copy of *Treasure Island* from its box and started flipping through the remaining pages. Maybe . . . *maybe* . . .

"Here it is!" I shook the book like a cheerleader with a pom-pom. "It was Captain Smollett. Right here. Chapter twelve. He said, 'We must go on, because we can't turn back'!"

"So Maxine plagiarized part of her speech from an old book." Kevin shrugged. "Big deal."

"Hold on, Kev," Elena said. "Gee might be right." She held up one finger. "*S* for *Scholar's.*" She held up a second finger. "*T* for *To.*" She held up a third and final finger. "And *E* for *Eyes. S-T-E.*"

Max's eyebrows drew together in confusion. "You kids stumped me. What does *S-T-E* have to do with that book?"

Edgar looked equally confused. And Sauce probably would've looked confused too, if he hadn't been snoring.

But I knew exactly what Elena meant. "*S-T-E,*" she said. "For *Stevenson.*"

I held up the book. The grin spreading across my face was mirrored on Elena's. "More specifically," I said, "Robert Louis Stevenson—the author of *Treasure Island.* Max, is there some connection between Robert Louis Stevenson and the Van Houtens?"

Max scratched his lower lip. "Nothing I can think of," he said. "But there *is* a family cemetery on the estate. What if there's a 'Stevenson' in there?"

Naturally, the next thing we did was visit some dead people.

11

We hustled outside. The cemetery sat along the north side of the house. There were some angel statues and a few dozen moss-covered tombstones that poked from the weeds like crooked teeth in need of an orthodontist. There was also a mausoleum, which is a building used to bury people aboveground. It basically looked like an oversized garden shed made from large stone blocks. Weeds sprouted between the blocks, and two fancy granite pillars framed a wooden door.

"Check the gravestones," Kevin said, trying to take charge. "Look for *Stevenson.*"

Of course, we were already busy doing exactly that. Max, who'd said he needed a break from the house, had come with us too.

We went grave by grave, stone by stone, Sauce

sniffing and snuffling, the rest of us examining the names. Some of the graves dated all the way back to the early 1800s—nearly as old as Elmwood itself. Most of the stones were hard to read because they were so worn and weathered, but we could make out enough of the faded letters to know one thing for certain—no Stevensons had ever been buried in the Van Houten family cemetery. Nor Roberts or Louises, for that matter.

"This doesn't make any sense!" Kevin tore out a handful of weeds and hurled it at a half-fallen gravestone. "*This* is the pinnacle of the town. *This* is Maxine's citadel. The fortune has to be here somewhere!"

Edgar placed one hand over his heart and flung his other arm out dramatically. "As the Bard so wisely imparted, 'All that glisters is not gold; / Often have you heard that told. / Many a man his life hath sold / But my outside to behold. / Gilded tombs do worms enfold.'"

Kevin huffed a short, sharp breath out his nose. "We need *Stevenson* right now, Edgar. Not Shakespeare."

"But maybe we need to *think* like Shakespeare," Edgar said.

"What do you mean?" Max and I asked simultaneously.

Edgar shrugged. "Shakespeare's poetic. Lots of times poems aren't literal. Instead of *pinnacle* talking about an actual high point, it could be the highest level of an achievement or something."

Elena's thumbs flew across her phone screen. "Check this out," she said. "*Citadel* can mean more than a fortress. It can also mean a stronghold of something, like a 'citadel of knowledge.'"

I bobbed my head. Now we were getting somewhere! "The word *Scholar's* is in the clue," I said. "And a scholar's citadel would be a citadel of knowledge, wouldn't it? So what do you think a scholar's 'citadel of knowledge' actually is . . . ?"

But my reporter's brain had landed on the solution before I had even finished asking.

I smiled at Max and my friends. Then Elena and Edgar both shouted right along with me: *"The library!"*

A few minutes later, we arrived—out of breath—in front of the Elmwood Public Library, which sat across the street from Burkhart Bakery and kitty-corner to Van Houten Park. Max had stayed behind, saying he needed to keep cleaning, and asked us to keep him updated. I tied Sauce's leash to the library's bike rack and handed him a treat. No *way* was he going to pull the whole bike rack over.

Kevin was the only one who thought we were wasting our time. "If there's a clue in a book, someone obviously would have checked the book out from the library and found it by now," he said. "Just consider the mathematical odds."

"Probably true," Edgar said. "But they might not have known what they were looking at."

"And, Kev," Elena said, "you gotta admit it all fits— the quote from *Treasure Island*, the *S-T-E* for Robert Louis Stevenson, the library as a citadel. The library's gotta have at least one copy of the book, and it may hold the next clue. We can't ignore it."

Kevin didn't look convinced, but he followed the rest of us inside.

Mrs. Sánchez—the round-faced, rosy-cheeked librarian—wore a bright yellow blouse with turquoise and orange flowers embroidered around the collar. As always, she wore matching glasses, which today were a thick-framed turquoise pair that also matched her large hoop earrings. She greeted us as soon as we stepped through the door: "Ah, if it isn't four of my favorite patrons! How may I help you today?"

Elena didn't mince words. "We need *Treasure Island*," she said. "Please."

"A wonderful choice." Mrs. Sánchez pointed to a nearby row. "End of the aisle, top shelf."

We quickly found four copies and each grabbed one.

"This edition is only ten years old," Kevin said, shoving his paperback copy back on the shelf. "Maxine was already dead."

Edgar and I found that our copies were the same as Kevin's.

Then Elena flipped to the front of her copy, which was a hardcover edition with an old-book smell that reminded me of the newspaper office. "1985. This is old enough!"

We crowded around. The slightly yellowed pages crinkled as Elena turned them slowly, one by one. We looked for notes in the margins. Underlined words. Circled letters. Anything Maxine might have left behind. Elena even peeled back the protective plastic sleeve to see if anything lay hidden beneath the cover. Nothing, nothing, nothing, and nothing.

"We're wasting our time here," Kevin said.

"Chill." Elena slid the book back on the shelf with the others. "Just because your idea wasn't right, Kev . . ." Her voice trailed off, and she studied the four side-by-side copies of *Treasure Island.* She pointed to the stickers on their spines. "*S-T-E*-point-eight-two-three. There's that whole *S-T-E* thing again. . . ."

"The call number," I said, glancing at the STE.823 on the spine of each book. "That tells you where it should be shelved, but that doesn't help us. We've already found the book, and it doesn't have any clues inside."

That's when Kevin surprised me. Instead of grumbling again, he leaned forward and squinted at one of the books. His lips started moving, and I could just make out his whispered words: "One, two, three . . ."

Kevin counted to eight. Then to two. Then to three.

"Wow, Kev," Elena said, grinning at me. "You really *are* a math wizard. You auditioning for the Count on *Sesame Street*?"

Edgar snorted a laugh.

"Tease me all you want," Kevin said. "But check this out. In the clue, *Scholar's* has eight letters, *To* has two, and *Eye* has three. *S-T-E*-eight-two-three."

"It *can't* be a coincidence," Edgar said.

Elena reached over for a high five from Kevin. "The Count saves the day!"

Kevin grinned.

I pulled out the clue and read the first two lines out loud. We hadn't discussed those yet. " 'Life's not a matter of holding good cards, but of playing a poor hand well.' How does that go with the rest of the clue?"

"Poker night at the library?" Elena guessed.

"There are other types of cards," Edgar said. "Bingo cards . . . credit cards . . ." He pulled a card from his pocket, where he'd copied down some Shakespeare he was memorizing. "Index cards . . ."

I gasped. "That's it!"

The other GEEKs looked at me.

"The book's call number—*S-T-E*-eight-two-three. We don't need the *book*. We need the *catalog card*!"

Elena squinted at me like I'd sprouted a horn from the middle of my forehead and called myself a unicorn. "Um . . . what's that mean in English, Gee?"

"Before libraries had computers, if you wanted to find a book, you used the card catalog. You looked up a book by its title, author, or subject, and the catalog card would give you its call number. That's how you knew where the book was shelved. We know we want to find *Treasure Island*. So now we have to find the catalog card."

We rushed to the checkout desk, where Mrs. Sánchez was trying to repair a copy of *Goodnight Moon* that looked like it had been mauled by a grizzly.

"Mrs. Sánchez," Kevin said, "where's the card catalog?"

Mrs. Sánchez set down her roll of tape, looking surprised. "Oh, we got rid of that years ago. You know how it is—everything's computerized these days. All digital this and digital that."

"Oh," Kevin said. His chin dropped to his chest. "Well . . ."

"Why are you interested?" Mrs. Sánchez asked, clearly still puzzled.

The catalog card had disappeared, and with it, so had our hope of finding the next clue—which had most of us feeling too defeated to respond. But Edgar and his acting skills came to the rescue. Somehow he managed to smile as he said, "We're interested in the history of Elmwood and the library, and the card catalog seems very . . . *historical.*"

Mrs. Sánchez laughed. "Really, it was only taking up space." She took off her glasses and polished them on her blouse. "But if you're interested in the history of the library—and even in those old catalog cards—there *is* one person you might want to visit. . . ."

At Mrs. Sánchez's comment, my breathing stopped as suddenly as a printing press with a misspelled headline.

"Ms. Kaminski was the librarian here for decades," Mrs. Sánchez continued. "She loved this library more than life itself."

Thanks to my constant search for journalistic scoops, I knew most of the people in Elmwood, but I'd never heard of Ms. Kaminski. I released the breath I'd been holding and asked, "Does she still live around here?"

"Oh yes," Mrs. Sánchez said. She pressed some more tape onto *Goodnight Moon*. "She's getting along in years, but still sharp as a tack, as the saying goes. Visits the library every Monday at noon, like clockwork. Lives quite close, actually. Are you familiar with the little yellow cottage behind the Community Church?"

"On Maple Ridge Road?" Elena asked. "The place with all the flowers?"

Mrs. Sánchez's turquoise earrings swung when she nodded. "That's the one."

I looked from Elena to Edgar to Kevin. All their eyes shone with the same glimmer I felt in my own—the glimmer of new hope.

"I'm sure she'd love visitors," Mrs. Sánchez added. "Especially ones interested in the library." She smiled and made a shooing motion with *Goodnight Moon.* "Now, why don't you children go brighten another librarian's day?"

Ms. Kaminski's house was pale yellow with sky-blue shutters and a bright blue door. I'd noticed it before because it was about the only house in town that managed to have something blooming along the front walk in spring, summer, *and* fall. The smell of fresh cedar mulch hung in the air, and I didn't spot a single weed.

As we walked up the path, Elena pointed to some tall purple flowers. "Look! *Symphyotrichum novae-angliae!*"

Sauce sniffed one and sneezed.

Kevin pushed the doorbell. A short series of notes chimed musically from inside.

"Coming," someone called. The accented voice sounded familiar, but I couldn't figure out why. Then the door swung open. Which was when I discovered that Ms. Kaminski was the stooped, white-haired lady I'd nearly run over at the farmers market.

Ms. Kaminski looked down at Sauce, then up at the rest of us. Her blue eyes twinkled behind her thick glasses when she recognized me. "I told you this morning, dear, I'm right as rain. I may be as ancient as Methuselah, but it will take more than a minor collision to stop this old gal from dancing." To prove her point, Ms. Kaminski did some shuffling, arm-flapping thing that looked like a super-slow-motion chicken dance.

I had no clue who Methuselah was, but I got the idea.

"I'm glad you're okay," I said. "But we dropped by for something else. You see, we . . ." That's when I realized we'd been in such a hurry to get to Ms. Kaminski's, we hadn't actually come up with a plan for what to tell her. It wasn't like we could explain how we were hunting for the lost Van Houten fortune and needed the old library catalog card from *Treasure Island* to find the next clue. So what *could* I say?

Fortunately, Edgar's improv acting skills came to the rescue again. He stepped forward and bowed slightly. "Good afternoon, Ms. Kaminski," he said, all charm and innocence. There was something about his round face and mess of loopy red curls that would have made an angel look guilty standing next to him. "I'm Edgar Feingarten, and I'm pleased to make your acquaintance. My friends and I"—he swept his arm out, gesturing grandly to the rest of us—"are working on an article for the *Elmwood Tribune* concerning the history of the town library. One of our sources warned us that under no circumstances should such an article be undertaken unless we first consulted *your* lifetime of experience and expertise. Might you be willing to spare a moment of your day for us?"

When Edgar finished his monologue, Ms. Kaminski burst into a short, crackly laugh. She reached up with both wrinkly hands and pinched Edgar's cheeks. "My dear boy, you are a charmer, aren't you?" She gave his cheeks a gentle jiggle.

"Yeah, he's a total Prince Charming," Elena teased.

Edgar blushed. But this time he wasn't acting.

Ms. Kaminski took a step back and held open the door. "Do come in. All of you. Your doggy friend, too."

Sauce seemed to understand the invitation. He gave a short, happy bark and pushed his way past us, tail wagging, ears dragging. We followed him.

We walked into a tiny living room with striped, flowery wallpaper and a polished wooden floor. An ancient, boxy TV sat on an oak cabinet, and a small vase of flowers stood beside it. Open shelves on the ends of the cabinet held dozens and dozens of books, from paperbacks to older, leather-bound ones that reminded me of my writing journal.

Ms. Kaminski shuffled over to a blue armchair embroidered with green vines and little red roses. She looked at Sauce and patted her thighs. "Come here, boy. Keep an old gal company."

Sauce scrabbled onto Ms. Kaminski's lap and planted a wet, slurping kiss on her bony elbow.

As the other GEEKs and I settled onto Ms. Kaminski's couch and introduced ourselves, a plaque on the wall near the TV caught my eye. The plaque was from 1989, but it looked freshly polished. That wasn't what caught my attention, though. It was the *words* that had me interested—words I couldn't read.

At the same time that I pointed to the plaque and asked, "What's that say?" Kevin asked, "Can you tell us about the library?"

Ms. Kaminski seemed to skip past Kevin's request and gazed silently at the plaque for a long time. I held my breath. It was obvious Ms. Kaminski's mind had wandered to some far-off time and place. Even Elena—who *always* has something to say—kept quiet and waited. Then Ms. Kaminski began her story, which ended up answering my question *and* Kevin's.

13

"The words are Polish," Ms. Kaminski said, her voice thin and quiet as she looked at the plaque on her wall. "They are to honor my bravery during the Second World War, though I've always felt that gives me too much credit for simply caring about books."

Ms. Kaminski paused. A clock on the wall behind me tick-tick-ticked away, counting her memories.

I opened my notebook and pulled the pencil from my hair. Maybe this really *was* a story for the newspaper.

"You see," Ms. Kaminski continued, "I was a sixteen-year-old junior librarian in Warsaw, Poland, in 1939, when the Nazis invaded. I can still hear the planes buzzing overhead, see the flash of bombs, smell the black smoke thickening the air." Ms. Kaminski stared at her lap, slowly stroking Sauce's long ears as she spoke. "The Polish army had no chance."

"So what did you do?" Elena asked, unable to stay quiet any longer.

"The Germans, they took so many lives. You'll know this of course, because it was the greatest tragedy of all. But they took other things too. Libraries and museums destroyed. Monuments razed. Our very culture was being torn from us." Ms. Kaminski's shoulders gave the tiniest of shrugs. "I was only one little sixteen-year-old girl. What could I do against Nazis with their tanks and guns and cruelty? So I fought them the only way I knew how—I saved books. Books they would have burned."

I wrote down Ms. Kaminski's story as she told us how she took trip after trip from the library to her home, carrying as many books as she dared, praying she didn't catch the eye of any Nazi soldiers. She packed books into her family's piano, hid them beneath the floorboards of the kitchen, even stuffed them up the chimney and endured a frigid winter because her family couldn't light a fire in the fireplace. She took hundreds of trips, saved thousands of books. And then the war finally ended.

"But," she said, "Poland still was not free." For the first time since she'd started talking, Ms. Kaminski looked up. Her eyes glistened behind her thick glasses.

"Although the Nazis had been defeated, both my parents had died during the war, and then Poland fell under the control of the Soviet Union. All that time, I kept the books. But eventually, it became too painful for me to stay. I put the books into the hands of another librarian and escaped to America to find a new life. Not many were so lucky."

"So how did you end up in Elmwood?" Kevin asked.

Ms. Kaminski smiled faintly. "A reading mistake."

"What do you mean?" Edgar asked.

"Unfortunately, even in America," Ms. Kaminski said, "the land of the free, I found prejudice. For a young Polish immigrant with an odd accent, finding work proved not simply difficult, but impossible. At least until I misread a bus route and got stranded in Elmwood, where I found myself accepting a cup of coffee from a stranger named Maxine Van Houten."

Ms. Kaminski continued to tell us her story, and I couldn't help but wonder how I'd lived in Elmwood my entire life and never known who she was. I promised myself I *would* write an article about her someday. However, for now I'll stick to the facts about how she ended up being Elmwood's librarian:

FACT #1: The Elmwood Public Library was brand-new and preparing for its grand opening.

FACT #2: The library did *not* yet have a librarian.

FACT #3: Maxine Van Houten decided, on the spot, that Ms. Kaminski absolutely *had to* become the town's librarian.

FACT #4: Ms. Kaminski accepted the job and has lived in Elmwood ever since.

When Maxine learned how Ms. Kaminski had saved books from the Nazis, she wrote to the authorities in Warsaw, Poland, telling them about Ms. Kaminski's bravery. Maxine never received a reply to her letter, and Ms. Kaminski didn't even know about it. At least not until two years after Maxine died.

In 1989, Ms. Kaminski explained, the Soviet Union began to collapse, and Poland became a democracy. A few years later, someone in the office of some Polish politician bigwig came across Maxine's decades-old letter. He even tracked down some of the books Ms. Kaminski had saved, which had ended up in libraries and museums. Some of them had been rare even before the Nazis had begun burning books.

The next thing Ms. Kaminski knew, she was on a plane to Poland, where she took part in a special ceremony and received the plaque. It was the first (and the last) time she'd returned to Poland since leaving many decades earlier.

Anyway, when Ms. Kaminski's voice trailed off at the end of her story, the only sounds in her living room were the clock on the wall and Sauce—who'd fallen asleep in her lap and started snoring.

After a moment, Ms. Kaminski gave an embarrassed laugh. "I'm sorry, my dears, I guess you've just learned how much an old gal can ramble when she has nearly one hundred years of life on which to reminisce." She adjusted her glasses. "Now, what was it you wanted to know about our precious town library?"

"It's clear you love the library," I said gently. "With the town's current struggles, we're afraid it might be shut down. So, just like you saved all those books during World War Two, we want to do our best to save the Elmwood library. You know, by"—I fiddled with my pencil, wishing I could give Ms. Kaminski the truth—"by writing our article for the newspaper and letting everyone know the library is vital to our town."

Ms. Kaminski sniffled. "I do love our library," she said, "and I'm glad Elmwood has children like you who care so deeply for it."

"You know, Ms. K," Elena said, "you've given us boatloads of great information. Gee's a real-deal journalist, and I bet she'll turn it into a terrific article. But I was wondering—do you maybe have a visual we could print with it? One of those old-fashioned book cards or something?"

"Oh, catalog cards!" Ms. Kaminski grunted as she lowered the still-snoring Sauce to the floor. "Now, you're going to think I'm a pack rat, but I couldn't let a piece of our town's library be destroyed simply because someone decided it was outdated." She braced her hands on the arms of her chair and stood.

Elena hopped to her feet. "Ms. K, does that mean—"

Ms. Kaminski shuffled over to the TV cabinet. That's when I noticed the wheels.

She pushed on one end of the cabinet, and it rolled to the side. Behind the cabinet was a square door.

"Silly of me, isn't it?" Ms. Kaminski said, pulling the door open. "Hiding things as if the Nazis still might come pounding on my door. But, you know, old habits . . ." She nudged me with her elbow. "Maybe you can leave this part out of your story, dear. Don't want folks thinking I'm batty."

I was too busy staring into the hidden cubby to respond. Stacks and stacks of narrow cardboard boxes sat there, with neat, cursive script on the end of each one: *Elmwood Library Card Catalog.*

14

"Is there a particular card you'd care to use for your article?" Ms. Kaminski asked.

"*Treasure Island!*" I blurted.

Ms. Kaminski smiled. "That's funny. It was one of Maxine's favorites." She pointed to a box near the bottom of a stack. "Edgar, my dear, would you be a chivalrous youth and procure that box?"

Edgar shifted the other boxes out of the way and pulled out the one Ms. Kaminski had indicated.

Kevin took a step forward, but Elena and I were closer. Elena popped the lid from the box. I flipped through the alphabetized contents. It only took a moment to find the card for *Treasure Island.*

"Let me see it," Kevin said, grabbing for the card as I slid it from the box.

I moved the card out of his reach, holding it up where all four of us could see it. I turned it this way and that, examining the front, the back, right side up, upside down. But there was nothing unusual about it at all. It just gave the book title, publication year, call number, and a short summary.

"There's nothing here," I murmured.

Ms. Kaminski gave a gentle cough. "I have a feeling there's more going on here than a news article about the library."

I shifted nervously from foot to foot. "Um . . . maybe?"

"Kind of," Kevin admitted.

"A little," Edgar added.

"But this has to be right," Elena muttered to herself. "Everything about the clue led us here. 'Life's not a matter of holding good cards, but of playing a poor hand well.' "

"Ah," said Ms. Kaminski. "I see you are true Stevenson fans."

"What do you mean?" I asked.

Ms. Kaminski looked at me, puzzled. "That quote is often attributed to him."

"*See?*" Elena cried. "This has to be right! The scholar's treasure . . . the highest pinnacle . . . the sour key." Then she gasped.

"That's it!" she shouted.

"*What?*" the rest of us asked.

101

She snatched the card out of my hand. "Ms. K, do you have some matches and a candle?"

"Oh, dearie," Ms. Kaminski said. "This old gal loves a mystery!" She shuffled off.

"Um, Elena," I asked when Ms. Kaminski was out of earshot, "you're not planning to start a fire or anything, are you?"

Elena shook her head. "Of course not! It's the poem! The line about a *sour key*. We never thought about the word *sour*. And what's the sourest thing you can think of?"

"Uh, expired milk?" tried Edgar.

"No, Dairy Boy!" Elena cried, shooting her hands up in the air. "Lemons! The clue *is* here; we just can't see it yet! This is *Secret Message Writing 101* stuff—the good ol' write-in-lemon-juice-then-heat-it-up-to-read-it trick."

Elena added some other stuff about carbon-based compounds, paper fibers, and the need for a heat source to promote oxidation, but I was really too excited to pay attention. If Elena was right, we were so close!

Fortunately, I didn't have long to wait. Ms. Kaminski came back with a book of matches and a fat white candle with a few streaks of dried wax running down the outside. "Here you go, dear," she said, handing them to me.

The other GEEKs and I looked at each other. We were on a supposed-to-be-secret treasure hunt but had already kind of blown our cover with Ms. Kaminski. Whatever Elena thought her science trick might reveal, could we afford to let Ms. Kaminski see it?

Ms. Kaminski must have spotted the nervousness on our faces. "Don't worry, dears," she said, "I won't ask. I trust you. What's a small town like this without trust? All we've got is each other." She looked us all in the eyes, then winked. "Though I sure wouldn't mind another visit and an explanation once your little adventure is over."

"You bet, Ms. Kaminski," said Edgar.

Ms. Kaminski gave a thin, crackly laugh and left us there, Elena holding the catalog card for *Treasure Island* and me holding the matches and the candle.

"Come on, Elena," Kevin said. "Whatever science stuff you're going to do, just do it."

"Don't get your undies in a wad, Kev. Science can't be rushed," Elena said. But she didn't waste any time lighting the candle, then holding the catalog card a couple of inches above the flame.

I held the candle and watched. Faint brown letters slowly appeared across the face of the card, as if burned there by magic: *MY GREATEST ACHIEVEMENT.*

Elena waved the card back and forth in front of the candle, but nothing else appeared.

"That's all we get?" Kevin said. "Three words?"

"What does it mean?" Edgar asked.

But before we could discuss the new clue, Kevin's phone buzzed. He glanced at the screen. "Shoot," he said. "Dinnertime. You know how my mom and dad are about family dinners."

Dinnertime? How'd it get to be so late?

My stomach rumbled, making me realize I hadn't eaten anything since the blueberry muffin at the farmers market. I checked my phone, which I'd had on silent all day. I winced. Seven unread texts from Mom.

Edgar and Elena checked their phones too. More of the same.

A moment later, we were all saying, "Thank you!" and "Goodbye!" and "We'll be back!" as Ms. Kaminski waved to us from her front step.

Out on the street, we had to split in four different directions.

"Let's meet at the Lookout tomorrow morning," I said. "Nine o'clock."

Kevin frowned. "I have church. . . ."

And after church service, I knew, would come Sunday school. Kevin wouldn't be free until the afternoon. No way could we wait that long to get back to work. We had a case to solve. A fortune to find! "We can catch you up when you get home."

"But—"

"Don't worry, Kev," Elena said. "We won't solve the *whole* thing without you."

Kevin looked like he wanted to argue, but his phone buzzed again. He scanned the message. "Fine," he said. "I have to get home. See you guys tomorrow afternoon."

He took off, and the other GEEKs did too.

I wished I could follow our newest lead and find the hidden fortune. But I had to get home like everyone else. Sauce and I turned toward White Bend Road. Whatever Maxine Van Houten's greatest achievement was, it would have to wait until morning.

I'd planned a dozen different apologies and excuses for not reading Mom's texts. It turned out I didn't need any of them.

After Sauce and I rushed through the printing room, pounded up the metal stairs, and burst into the apartment, I blurted, "Sorry, Mom. I know we're late!"

Mom stood with a pan of steaming lasagna, fresh from the oven. The heavenly scent of melting cheese and tomato sauce filled the air. "It's fine, Bean," she said. She set the lasagna on top of the stove and stared out the window. "I just . . . it's fine."

I should have been worried about how distracted Mom was, but I was distracted too. Plus, I was hungry.

We ate at the scuffed rectangular table that used to be the center of the newspaper's break room. Mom scooped a steaming square of lasagna onto my plate while I tore two hunks of warm bread from a foil-wrapped loaf. I slipped one of the hunks under the table to Sauce.

"You know," Mom said, "things will be tough around here with the factory closing."

"Mm-hm," I said, my mouth full of bread. In my mind I watched a candle flicker, a library catalog card held above the flame.

"It will be hard on the town."

"Mm-hm." I shoveled a forkful of lasagna into my mouth. The candle and card stayed in my mind as— slowly, ever so slowly—three words grew dark against the paper.

"Lots of people losing their jobs."

Mom's comment snapped me back into the moment. The risk of people losing their jobs was exactly why the GEEKs' treasure hunt had to succeed. As Mom twisted her napkin around and around, I wished I could tell her everything. Instead, I swallowed my mouthful of lasagna and asked, "What do you think Maxine Van Houten's greatest achievement was?"

Mom stopped twisting her napkin. "Huh?"

"Maxine Van Houten's greatest achievement. What do you think it was? With the Bamboozler getting made somewhere else and the factory about to close, I've just been wondering."

A tightness seeped away from Mom's shoulders, like maybe she was actually thankful for my sudden change of topic. She began to unwind her napkin. "It depends who you ask, I suppose. Some townspeople might say the nature preserve. Or the creation of the park downtown, or Bamboozleland, before it closed. Maxine herself might have had some totally different answer—her children or something like that. If you asked someone outside town, they would probably say her greatest achievement was the Bamboozler."

At Mom's mention of Elmwood's best-known toy, I ground my teeth. "If the Bamboozler was Maxine's greatest achievement, it isn't fair that her kids sold it off! It should benefit the town Maxine loved."

"I agree, Bean," Mom said. "It's a shame what's happening. However, that doesn't erase all the other things Maxine did for the town."

I forced myself to take another bite of lasagna. I knew Mom was right. In fact, I knew it even better than she did, because *I* knew about Maxine's hidden treasure. But my worries about the new clue made it hard to think straight.

Mom chewed slowly on a bite of lasagna, then set her fork down beside her plate. She swallowed, staring into her own lap. "With everything going on, Bean, there's something I've been wanting to talk to you about. Since the factory is closing and all"—she picked up her napkin and started folding it and unfolding it beside her plate—"maybe it will actually lead to some good."

Journalists are usually pretty rational people, but just then my mom wasn't making any sense. "Mom, how can you say that? Elena's mom is going to lose her job. So is Kevin's dad. Plus all the other people who work in the factory."

"I know, Bean. I'm not trying to say those things are good. They're not. People losing their jobs is horrible. But . . . well, the paper's been struggling for a long time. Maybe this is the push we need—the final nudge to start over. You know, somewhere new."

"Start over?" I shoved back from the table, accidently stepping on Sauce's tail. He yipped. "You can't be serious!"

"I'm not rushing any decisions, but we have to consider—"

"We don't have to consider anything!"

"The town barely has enough people to support the newspaper as it is," Mom said, her voice level, reasonable, infuriating. "If the factory closes, then what?"

It wasn't like I hadn't been thinking and worrying about those things already. I'd seen the FINAL NOTICE paper on her desk. But, somehow, having my mom actually speak the words aloud made them more real, more terrifying.

"Remember my cousin Frankie?" Mom asked. "She's

been working in Boston with the Beantown Lifestyle Living website for the past year and says there's a job opening. It would be a different type of writing than the newspaper, but it would be a regular paycheck. A new challenge. A new adventure."

"I don't want a new challenge *or* a new adventure." My face grew warm. "How can you even think about moving? You grew up in Elmwood too."

"Frankie's apartment in Boston isn't huge, but there's room for the two of us."

Boston? With no Lookout? No *Elmwood Tribune*? No GEEKs? I squeezed my eyes shut and swiped away the tears. I wouldn't cry. Wouldn't, wouldn't, wouldn't.

"Frankie says we can live with her until we get on our feet." Mom reached across the table.

I yanked my hand away. As a journalist, I'm used to focusing on facts, not emotions. But this was too much. "No!" I shouted. "I won't live in a city! I won't leave my friends!"

"It's not for certain, Bean. It's just—"

"You can't make me leave!" Then I did something I'd never done before—I stomped away from the table and to my room.

"Gina Bean . . . ," my mom called after me, but she didn't try to stop me.

Sauce chugged past and slipped into my bedroom right before I slammed my door.

I collapsed face-first onto my bed, crying. Sauce hopped up beside me and burrowed his cold snout under my arm, licking the tears from my cheeks. I hugged him tight.

I'm not sure how long I lay there, but eventually, my tears stopped and Sauce's snores started, his nose still nuzzled against my cheek. I stayed facedown, my mind churning over everything my mom had said. Now, solving the clue was more important than ever. I *had* to figure out Maxine Van Houten's greatest achievement!

And that's when I thought of Max.

We were supposed to keep him updated on our progress. Would he have an idea about his grandmother's greatest achievement? I untangled myself from Sauce and pulled out my phone.

"Hello?" Max answered. "Gina?"

"We've got another clue, Max." I kept my voice quiet, hoping my mom wouldn't overhear. "I think maybe you can help."

I explained all about the catalog card and the lemon juice and the hidden three-word message. I told Max about my guesses at Maxine's "greatest achievement." But when I asked for his ideas . . .

"I'm sorry, Gina," he said. "That's great news about the new clue, but I just don't know. I didn't get to spend a lot of time with my grandmother. I don't have any guesses other than the ones you already said."

"Oh." I couldn't keep the disappointment from my voice. "I'd hoped—"

"I'll keep thinking about it, though. And I can look around the mansion some more. That clue gives me something to focus on." Max paused. "And, Gina?"

"Yeah?"

"Don't give up. You kids are doing an amazing job."

I mumbled my thanks and hung up, trying to regain some of the hope I'd felt earlier in the day. I pulled out my laptop and typed in a search: *Maxine Van Houten achievements*.

Then I grabbed my notebook. I had to solve this. I had to save Elmwood. And I was running out of time.

Saturday, September 18

Observations & COGITATIONS

(Maxine Van Houten—Greatest Achievements)

- ~~Invented the Bamboozler~~
  ↝ TOO OBVIOUS
- Established the Van Houten Nature Conservatory
- Holds over 1,000 patents for toys & other inventions
- First woman on the cover of TOY INVENTOR magazine
  ↝ GIRL POWER!
- Longtime CEO of Van Houten Toy & Game Co.
  ↝ TOOK THE COMPANY OVER FROM HER HUSBAND'S UNCLE, SO IS IT TOTALLY *HER* ACHIEVEMENT?
- ~~Mother of Alice, Cynthia, and Harold, Jr.~~
  ↝ JUST LOOK HOW THEY TURNED OUT!
- Met Albert Einstein in 1950
  ↝ ELENA'S GOING TO LOVE THIS FACT!

16

A cool breeze rustled its way through the preserve as Edgar, Elena, and I sat in the Lookout on Sunday morning. I yawned. It had been a long night of research, but I wasn't sure if I had actually made any progress.

"This is great, Gina," Edgar said, looking over my shoulder at the pages of notes I had taken on Maxine. "There has to be something in all of this that connects to the clue."

"But what?" I asked glumly.

Elena smiled. "Chin up, Gee. I was doing some thinking of my own last night, and I got us covered. I figured out our next step."

"Seriously?" I asked.

"Think about it. There's only one person who can tell us what Maxine's greatest achievement was." Elena paused and arched her eyebrows. She sat back and crossed her arms, smiling smugly.

"Fine, Elena, I give," I said. "Just tell us."

Elena threw out her arms. "Maxine!"

"Whoa, whoa, whoa," Edgar said. "If you're planning a séance, I'm outta here."

"Actually, Edge, we can stay in this realm of existence. All we need is Maxine's office."

"But Alice totally ransacked her office, remember?" Edgar asked.

"Not the office at the manor," Elena said. "The one at the *factory*. After Maxine died, the new CEO built a new office, and Maxine's was left alone, like a shrine or museum to honor Maxine's memory. I got to go inside back in fourth grade when I tagged along with my mom on Take Your Kid to Work Day."

"Aren't you overlooking a couple of facts?" I ticked them off on my fingers. "One, it's Sunday, so the factory's closed. Two, we're kids. It's not like we can walk up and knock on the factory door and—"

"I know I'm usually the science kid. But for today, I decided to expand my skill set." Elena reached into her back pocket. "Voilà!" She whipped something from her jacket and dangled it in front of us like she was a hypnotist.

My mouth dropped open. "You *stole* your mom's work ID?"

"*Stole* is such a negative word, Gee." Elena stuffed the ID back into her pocket. "I prefer 'ignorance-based borrowing.'"

Edgar was shaking his head. "You remember that your dad is Elmwood's chief of police, right, Elena? You can't—"

"I can," said Elena, suddenly serious. "Because if I don't—if *we* don't find this treasure . . . my dad won't be Elmwood's police chief anymore, because there won't be an Elmwood. My mom won't have an ID badge for the factory, because it'll be an empty pile of bricks."

Edgar nodded. "Okay, Elena," he said. "You're right. Gina? You in?"

Elena's eyes were shining now, reminding me that I wasn't the only one here with everything to lose.

I stared at my notes, doubting they held the answers we needed, wondering if maybe Maxine's old office really did hold the key. I sighed. "We'd have to be extra careful. . . ."

I expected her to greet this statement with an eye roll or a joke, but for once, she couldn't seem to muster one. "We will, Gee," Elena said, blinking away the worry from her eyes. "Promise."

Elena sat on her bike and rested her elbows on the windowsill of the tiny guardhouse at Van Houten Toys. I stopped behind Edgar and tried to make myself invisible inside my hoodie.

"Hey, Cy," Elena said, sweet as Mrs. Dupree's apple pie. "Can you believe my mom forgot her reading glasses at work?" Elena shook her head. "Then she decided we should use *our* young legs to fetch them, since she's getting so old."

Cy laughed. "Better watch it. I ain't so young myself."

Elena winked. "You don't look a day over twenty."

This was a total lie. Cy Porter was bald as a pumpkin and his only remaining hair—his shaggy eyebrows and hairy arms—was white. But all of Elena's sweetness had the desired effect.

"All right, you kids can go in. But be fast. Guard shift changes in an hour. Need you out before Bernie replaces me." Cy pushed a button, and the heavy gate split down the middle, clanking and squeaking as it rolled to the sides.

The three of us biked and bumped across the parking lot's uneven pavement, which seemed to have more cracks than concrete. The factory itself was a four-story brick building that could fit at least three of Elmwood High's football field inside. Above the arched, glassed entrance, the once-colorful VAN HOUTEN TOY & GAME CO. sign was faded, and a bird's nest sprouted from the crook of the V.

We hopped off our bikes, and Elena swiped her mom's ID through a scanner beside the door.

Beep.

A light on the scanner blinked from red to green.

Click.

"C'mon," Elena said.

We were in.

17

Other than the faint glow of a few emergency lights, the foyer was dark. In the middle, a supersized metal replica of a Bamboozler sat on a low pedestal rising from the center of a broken fountain.

This Bamboozler was at least ten feet around, and instead of brightly colored plastic rods, it was made from a mix of now-tarnished brass, bronze, and silver. It was actually pretty cool. A few pennies and nickels still littered the fountain's dusty, dried-up bottom.

We headed into the heart of Van Houten Toys.

The squeak of our sneakers echoed as we passed through the cavernous main floor of the factory. Thick steel beams crisscrossed the ceiling four stories above our heads, and the machines that cranked out Bamboozlers and other toys six days a week stood shadowy, towering, and silent in the dim light. Large bins held piles and piles of the plastic rods and other pieces needed to assemble new Bamboozlers.

Elena led us from the main floor, up a flight of stairs, and down a short hall. At the end of the hall stood a single doorway, which was closed off by an old wooden door with peeling paint and a large window. That's when Edgar spotted the problem.

"There's no card scanner." Edgar pointed to the very ordinary lock of the very ordinary door. "Now what?"

"We could pick it," I said. We'd already come this far. . . .

Elena gave me a surprised look that quickly turned to admiration. "That's the spirit, Gee!"

"Does anyone know how to pick a lock?" Edgar asked, staring at Elena.

"Why would you assume *I* know?" she asked. "My dad arrests criminals. He doesn't bring them around for dinner. Now, if you wanted me to *dissolve* the lock . . ."

"The lock to the newspaper office always used to freeze up," I said. "We couldn't get the key to open it, so we had to use bobby pins. It's kind of the same thing, right?"

"It's worth a try. Either of you have something long and pointy?" Elena looked at Edgar and grinned. "Other than the top of Edge's head, that is."

"Very funny," Edgar said as we searched our pockets. Together, we came up with a pack of bubble gum, a tube of lip balm, three hair ties, and some pocket lint.

We jiggled the doorknob a few times, peered through the window, and stared at the lock awhile. We needed to get into that office. And we needed to do it fast.

"I have an idea!" Edgar said. He took off down the stairs and returned a minute later grasping a few brightly colored plastic sticks.

"Bamboozler pieces!" I said. "Edgar, you're brilliant!"

Edgar handed a couple of rods to me, and I got to work, trying to remember how Mom and I used to get the office door open. I stuck one rod in the top part of the lock and held it steady. Then I worked the second rod into the bottom of the lock and started wiggling and jiggling it. "Come on, come on," Elena said behind me. "Open up for Mama Locksmith."

I worked for a full minute before Edgar cleared his throat. "Gina? Are you sure you know—"

Click.

Yes!

"Score one for Mama Locksmith!" Elena cried as the door swung open. "Didn't know you had it in you, Gee." She slapped me on the back as she entered the office.

The doorway was a time machine, whisking us back to 1987. Framed pictures hung on the walls, including a black-and-white photo of a young Maxine standing beside a smiling Albert Einstein. An ancient, boxy, tan computer sat in the middle of a large wooden desk, a handful of file folders and design sketches spread out beside it. On the front corner of the desk, pens and pencils stuck out from a holder made to look like a Bamboozler. Behind the desk sat an office chair with a cracked black leather seat and backrest. A thick layer of dust covered everything.

"I'll check the desk," Elena said. Then she pointed to a couple of steel file cabinets along one wall. "Edge, Gee—look in those. There must be *something* around here about Maxine's greatest accomplishment."

Edgar and I tugged open drawers and riffled through the files. Once in a while, one of us would pull out a file folder and search it more carefully. Elena was doing the same sort of search of Maxine's desk. I was the first of us to find anything.

"Check this out," I said. "She was writing her auto-biography!" I held up a thick stack of typed pages. The front page said:

A Life Well Lived: My Story
by Maxine Van Houten

"Let's divvy up the pages and look for anywhere she talks about her 'greatest achievement,'" I said.

I handed Elena and Edgar each about a third of the pile, then started scanning my own share of the stack.

Maxine had written about her time in college . . . about meeting and marrying Harold Van Houten . . . about her growing family. But there was no mention of a "greatest achievement" and no time to keep hunting. If we didn't get out of there soon, Cy would get suspicious.

I was about to suggest we just take the pages with us, when Edgar blurted, "Hey, look!" He wasn't even reading his pages. Instead he was pointing at one of the framed pictures on the wall.

Elena and I rushed over to see, but it was only a poster and program from a long-ago performance of *Our Town* at the Elmwood Theater. Scrawled in one corner of the playbill, someone had written: *Thank you for bringing back our theater, Maxine!*

"Isn't this amazing?" Edgar gushed. He was practically dancing. "The actual playbill *and* a copy of the program from the reopening of the Elmwood Theater! I remember my parents telling me about—"

"Focus, Edgar," I said.

"—going to the show. The original theater was built during the Gilded Age, in the late eighteen hundreds, but it had—"

"Edgar, we need clues."

"—totally started to fall apart and was going to be torn down, so in the 1980s, when the Bamboozler was taking off as a favorite toy all around the world, Maxine completely updated the theater, then reopened it in 1983 with a performance of *Our Town,* and Maxine even played the role of the play's narrator, and—oh, man, I wish I could have—"

"EDGAR!"

Edgar's racing, rambling history lecture screeched to a halt. "Huh?"

I was about to tell him to get back to concentrating on Maxine's autobiography, when . . . "Wait," I said. "Bringing back the theater was a pretty huge accomplishment, wasn't it? Could *that* be what we're looking for?"

"Hold on," Elena said. "I think one of these chapters was about the theater. I skipped over it to get to the part about Einstein. . . ." She shuffled through her pages of the autobiography. For a few seconds, there was only the sound of riffling paper and then . . . "Aha!" Elena stabbed a finger at one of the pages. "Right here! 'Of all my achievements in life, nothing I've accomplished has been without the work and support of so many others who have surrounded me. However, the one thing I will take full credit for is my performance in *Our Town*. When you step onstage, it is up to you and you alone to bring your character to life. That role, perhaps, was my greatest *personal* achievement.'"

Elena and I stared at each other, then the poster of *Our Town.*

"What if . . . ," I started.

But before I could finish, Elena yanked the picture frame off the wall and tugged off the back.

"Careful," Edgar said. "That's Elmwood theatrical history!"

Elena didn't say anything. She just pulled the program out of the frame and began flipping through it. The list of scenes . . . the cast list and production crew . . . the pages of bios for the cast members . . .

Then there it was, on the same page as Maxine's bio and in the same tidy type as the other clues—another poem.

All the world is one big stage;

the audience is rapt.

The spotlight shines so brightly in

the place where you first act.

Forbidden vanity focuses

and prompts you to reflect.

There is a key that's out of place

from Elmwood's architect.

18

I wrapped Edgar in a massive hug and said, "I'm sorry for ever wishing you'd shut up about the theater!"

"What?" Edgar scratched his head.

"Never mind." I waved him off. "The important thing is that this clue must be sending us to the theater, right?"

Edgar and Elena agreed. We quickly straightened up the mess we'd made in the office and hustled out of the factory, nearly bashing into Cy as we burst from the foyer.

"Whoa," Cy said. "Careful." He rubbed a hand under his lumpy nose. "Glad I found you. I'm about to go off shift."

"Sorry," Elena said. "My mom's desk was a mess. But

we finally found her glasses." She pulled a pair of sunglasses from her pocket.

Cy's forehead wrinkled. "I thought you said it was her reading glasses."

"Oh, *yeah*," Elena said, stretching the *yeah* out for about five seconds. "You heard of these? They're these cool glasses that tint if it gets really bright. They're light-sensitive."

Cy squinted. "Light-sensitive reading glasses? Can I see those?"

"No," Elena said quickly. "I mean, I wish you could, but we're in kind of a hurry! Mom was really psyched to read the newspaper! Some other time, okay?"

Cy still looked confused as we climbed onto our bikes, but he didn't ask any more questions.

Edgar's a natural actor, and Elena was proving to be pretty good herself. As we quickly pedaled away, I hoped my innocent smile was at least half as good as theirs.

When we got to the theater, we quickly realized there was no easy way in. The front doors were secured with a huge padlock. No way was I getting that thing open. As Elena and I studied the building, Edgar kept up a running commentary on the theater's history: "Maxine restored the theater in the early 1980s, but then a big fire gutted it a couple of years later. Maxine started the repairs, but they weren't done before she died, and the town didn't have the money to finish. That's why it got condemned. I've seen photos of the inside from before the fire. It was amazing! Maybe if we find the fortune, then—"

"Guys! Hey, guys!"

Kevin was cutting across the corner of Van Houten Park, trotting toward the theater, chomping on a burger from the Maple Leaf.

As soon as Kevin crossed the street, Elena let him have it: "Jeez, Kev, can't you see we're working the case here? It's kind of important to lay low when I'm within sight of the police station!"

"Well, if you guys ever checked your phones, maybe I would have known what was going on!" Kevin said. "I've been looking for you all over town."

I pulled out my phone and checked the notifications. I didn't need to be a journalist to figure out why Kevin was so upset.

FACT #1: It was one-thirty p.m., and Kevin's church never went *that* late.

FACT #2: He had texted me nine times after getting home from church, and I'd never replied.

FACT #3: Then he'd called me four times, and I'd never answered.

"Sorry," I said. "We got distracted." But before I could tell Kevin about our new clue, shouting and laughter came from across the street.

"Hey, *GEEKs*!" Sophina Burkhart called. She was just leaving Burkhart Bakery, giggling minions in tow. "What are you doing over there?"

"None of your business," Elena snapped.

"You're right. I've got a busy afternoon anyway. Just going to deliver these freshly baked cookies to all the members of our sixth-grade class. A little reminder to vote for Sophina."

"Bribery is not democracy!" Kevin shouted. He shook his hamburger in Sophina's direction.

I shook my head at him. "Don't let Sophina distract you."

"I just want a fair election."

"Kev, we have a mystery to solve," Elena said.

Edgar patted Kevin's shoulder. "Yeah, you can worry about your campaign later. Right now, we need to save our town."

Kevin ground his teeth but then his eyes widened. "Hold on a second," he said, his voice squeaking with excitement. "What if I used my campaign to encourage kids to pull together and save Elmwood? Cake pops and cookies can't compete against the future of our town!"

"That's great, Kev. Now—"

"I'll prepare a speech for the farmers market next Saturday. It'll be perfect! You guys can help me publicize it, so people actually show up. I'll remind the other kids about our shared history in this town and our power to change the world, then—"

Elena waved her arms like she was a stranded castaway trying to signal a plane. "Kev, listen. We. Solved. The. Clue."

Kevin frowned. "You solved it without me?"

"Only partway," Edgar said. He nodded toward the theater. "We think the next answer's inside there."

Elena and Edgar started to tell Kevin all about what we'd done at the factory. That's when I noticed the man across the street.

The man stood at the edge of the park's flower garden, smoking a cigarette. Stringy gray hair poked from beneath his Yankees cap, and his belly bulged over his belt. He didn't seem to be watching us exactly, but he *did* keep glancing in our direction.

Nobody wearing a Yankees cap belonged this deep in Red Sox country.

What if the man knew about the fortune? What if he was eavesdropping?

"*Psst,*" I hissed. "Lower your voices." I turned my

back to the man, then pointed with my thumb over my shoulder so only my friends could see what I was doing. "Don't look, but maybe we should take our conversation somewhere else."

Of course they all looked.

"I told you not to look!" I said, turning back around too.

The man seemed focused on the rosebushes in the park, examining one of the roses as he took a drag on his cigarette.

"This treasure hunt's making you paranoid, Gee."

"No one else even knows about Maxine's treasure," Kevin added.

Elena and Kevin were probably right. But still . . . "Shouldn't we play it safe?" I asked.

"Follow my lead," Edgar said. He strolled down the steps and along the sidewalk.

I peeked over my shoulder right before we rounded the corner. The flower garden was only weeds and flowers, no Yankees Man.

There was an exit at the rear of the theater, and we were hidden from view in the deserted alley. Flies buzzed around an old, empty dumpster.

The back door was locked too.

"Now what?" I asked, feeling defeated.

"Well . . . there is the window," said Edgar, pointing up.

The rest of us followed his gaze to a window two stories up. There was a narrow gap between the window and the frame. Someone had left it open, just barely.

"I can do it," said Elena. "I'll just climb the drainpipe." She took off her jacket and tied it around her waist. Her T-shirt had a picture of a bubbling test tube with a crown on top and said: *Why be a PRINCESS when you can be a SCIENTIST?*

"Are you nuts?" I said. The drainpipe was rusty and bent and coming loose from the brick wall.

"It's not like we have another way in," Elena argued. "What're we gonna do? Go to the town administrator and say, 'Excuse me, Mr. Wright, would you please unlock the condemned theater so four GEEKs can search for lost treasure?'"

Before any of us could come up with an argument, Elena grabbed the drainpipe, stuck her feet against the wall, and started to climb.

Edgar, Kevin, and I grouped below Elena as she shimmied upward.

Edgar grimaced. "I probably shouldn't have mentioned the window. . . ."

I wanted to shout encouragement but didn't want to risk distracting her. I settled for thinking: *Don't fall, don't fall, don't fall.*

Halfway up, the pipe groaned under Elena's weight. *Don't fall.*

She kept climbing.

Three quarters of the way up, a few bits of brick crumbled away, skittering down the wall.

Don't fall.

She kept climbing.

I held my breath as Elena drew level with the window. It had a narrow, cement ledge. She kept one foot planted on the wall and stretched the other toward the ledge.

Don't fall.

Elena looked down at us.

Don't fall.

She reached for the window to push it open wider.

Don't fall.

And that's when the drainpipe gave an awful screech.

19

"The drainpipe is giving out!" Kevin cried at the same time that Elena shifted her weight off the pipe and onto the window ledge.

The rest of us shot out of the way as the ancient pipe came crashing down.

When we looked up again, Elena was shimmying in through the window.

Her sneakers were the last thing to disappear from sight. Then we heard a thud followed by a loud "Ow!"

"Are you okay?" I yelled.

"Eh, I'm all right. Just twisted my ankle" came a muffled reply.

"Yes!" Kevin pumped his fists above his head.

"She made it!" Edgar grabbed my hands and started dancing in circles. "She actually made it!"

We were still celebrating when Elena popped open the back door and said, "You GEEKs coming in before someone calls the cops to report bad dancing?"

The theater was dark, and the smell of smoke from the long-ago fire still hung in the air. We used the flashlights on our phones as we climbed a short flight of stairs to the backstage area, Elena limping slightly from her twisted ankle. The floorboards creaked. We dodged around one section that had rotted away under the leaking roof.

It was obvious the theater had been neglected for a long time, but when we pushed past the thick curtain separating the backstage from the main stage, I couldn't stop the "whoa" that escaped my lips.

Even in the skimpy lights of our phones, the theater was amazing. A balcony with an ornately carved railing overlooked the main floor. Above that, a row of lights hung from the bottom of a catwalk, which also had a large spotlight sitting on a platform in the middle.

I pulled out our latest clue.

"Right there in the third line," Kevin said. "'The spotlight shines so brightly.' What if we have to use the spotlight to find the next clue?"

"Good call, Kev." Elena limped across the stage, heading toward the balcony stairs. "I'll climb up and check it out."

"Not a chance." Kevin stepped in front of Elena and

pointed at her ankle. "You're hurt. As a sixth-grade class presidential candidate, I need to be willing to lead by example. I can climb." His voice shook a little as he said this, but Kevin headed to the rear of the auditorium and up to the balcony. At the back of the balcony, a ladder was mounted on the wall. Kevin hesitated a moment, then slowly, carefully, climbed up and started along the catwalk.

One step. Two. Three.

Kevin never should have looked down.

"Eeep," he squeaked. He dropped to his stomach and hugged the catwalk.

"Don't stop now, Kev!" Elena's voice boomed in the empty auditorium. "You're almost there!"

Kevin looked back at the ladder, then forward toward the spotlight. "I'm only a quarter of the way!" he protested.

"I was rounding up the fraction," Elena said. "Close is close."

"Use acting techniques," Edgar called. "Make your goal bigger than your fear!"

Kevin didn't budge.

Edgar tried again: "Focus *above* the light and crawl toward that spot."

Kevin's arms tightened around the catwalk.

"Picture me in my underwear!"

Elena made a gagging noise.

But apparently, an image of Edgar in his underpants was exactly the boost Kevin needed. He gave a nervous chuckle, and his grip on the catwalk loosened. He got onto his hands and knees and crawled, inch by inch, toward the spotlight.

Once he made it to the platform, I said, "Switch it on!"

Kevin swiveled the spotlight and flipped a switch.

Nothing happened.

"Hold on," Edgar said. "There's probably a master control." He disappeared backstage. A moment later, there was a *thunk,* followed by the spotlight blinding me and Elena.

"Are you *trying* to blind us, Kev?" Elena called.

"Sorry, sorry." He started to swivel the spotlight away.

"Wait!" I said. "The clue says 'the spotlight shines so brightly.' And a spotlight shines on—"

"'All the world is one big stage!'" Edgar boomed, as he thrust himself into the light. "Ah, that's better!"

"Right," I said, before Edgar could start belting a show tune. "So the stage is where we should look."

I blinked to clear my vision, and then we started searching.

Nothing looked out of place in the middle of the stage, so Kevin slowly rotated the spotlight. Still nothing—no trapdoors or secret loose floorboards or carved clues. Nothing.

"What else do we know?" I murmured. I looked down at the clue. " 'Forbidden vanity focuses and prompts you to reflect. . . .' "

"Reflecting?" Elena said. "Maybe like a mirror?"

"But there isn't a mirror onstage," Kevin argued.

"Wait! That's it!" Edgar jumped up from examining the stage's floorboards. "It's an old acting superstition — mirrors are forbidden onstage. A *forbidden vanity*!"

Kevin swept the spotlight around the walls of the theater, but there were no mirrors in sight. "If the mirror was for a specific show," he said, "it's hopeless. All the props are long gone."

"Ah, but there's one place we haven't looked yet," said Edgar.

He dashed offstage again and hauled on a thick rope. Pulleys creaked and squeaked overhead. The curtain that covered the stage's back wall slowly pulled aside, sending up a billow of dust that hung in the spotlight's glare. There — near the top of the rear brick wall, out of sight from the audience — was a tiny mirror hung at an angle.

"That's it!" Elena yelled. "Kev, shine the spotlight at the mirror!"

Kevin did.

The spotlight beam hit the mirror. The light bounced and focused on a single seat in the ninth row.

Elena, Edgar, and I ran to the floodlit seat, and Kevin

scrambled down from the catwalk far faster than he'd climbed up. Edgar crawled on the floor and looked underneath the seat. Elena pressed on the red velvet cushion and seat back, feeling for anything odd that might be hidden inside. Kevin tugged at the carved wooden armrests, trying to see if one of them was a secret lever or something.

It was just a seat—exactly like all the others in the auditorium. Except it was lit by a glowing spotlight.

"Angle measurements are important," Kevin said. "What if the mirror got bumped?"

As the other GEEKs broadened their search, I studied the floodlit seat one last time. Like the surrounding seats, it had fancy carvings in the wooden arms and along the top of the seat back. But . . .

"Look, guys." I pointed to the leaf carved along the seat's top edge. "The others look like elm leaves, but this one looks like a fan or something."

Elena examined it. "It's a carving of a gingko leaf," she said. "But that's just weird. Gingkoes are native to China, not New Hampshire. Plenty of American cities use them as decorative trees, but I've never seen any around town."

A quick check of the surrounding seats proved that only the floodlit seat had a gingko leaf. This had to be it! But where was the clue?

I ran my hand over the carving's bumps and ridges.

When I touched the right edge of the leaf, it moved slightly. I jiggled it some more and picked at it with my fingernails. The entire gingko leaf popped from the seat back and dropped into my hand, just as my heart leapt into my throat.

"I've got it!" I cried.

The other GEEKs huddled around. I flipped the leaf over, and Kevin shone his phone light on it. A number—11456—was carved into the back, and a quote curved its way around the edge in neat, tiny letters: *She is like a tree planted by streams of water that yields its fruit in season and its leaf does not wither.*

"Gee rocks it again!" Elena said.

Kevin waved his hand. "Don't forget I did the spotlight!"

"Don't worry, Kev, I know. And I got us in, and Edgar found the mirror. Team GEEK is kicking it!"

We all whooped and high-fived each other and danced in the aisle. Then the door at the rear of the auditorium banged open. A powerful flashlight shone in our faces. I shoved the gingko leaf into my pocket as a shadowy figure at the end of the aisle shouted, "Hey! What do you kids think you're doing in here?"

The Elmwood Tribune

Sunday, July 3, 1983

RESTORED THEATER CELEBRATES
OUR TOWN WITH "OUR TOWN"

By RAMONA LEE

Grover's Corners, New Hampshire, may be a fictional place, but it was brought to life in our very real town of Elmwood, New Hampshire, with Friday night's stunning performance of the Pulitzer Prize–winning play *Our Town.* To celebrate the grand reopening of the Elmwood Theater, the theater's benefactor—Maxine Van Houten—both selected and starred in the production.

Elmwood Theater, which first opened its doors in 1891, was one of the first theaters in the country to perform *Our Town*—a play that debuted in 1938 and which celebrates daily life in a small New Hampshire town much like Elmwood. This play provided the perfect backdrop to showcase the beautifully restored and reinvigorated Elmwood Theater. . . .

20

My mom wasn't smiling when she appeared outside the theater half an hour later. All the other GEEKs had already been picked up by their parents, so it was just me and Officer Yang standing awkwardly on the sidewalk.

"I thought I'd have at least a few more years before I had to worry about my daughter getting in trouble with the police," Mom said, her voice flat.

Officer Yang chuckled. "I don't think Gina and her friends were up to any real mischief, Ms. Sparks. Kevin tutored my daughter in math, and Elena is just about the best babysitter we've ever had. These are good kids."

"Well, I appreciate you letting them off with a warning."

"No problem. They're not delinquents, but they need to make better choices." Officer Yang turned to me. "Please remember what we talked about, Gina. Condemned properties are condemned for a reason—they're dangerous. And breaking and entering is illegal, regardless of whether a building is inhabited."

I nodded. It was a good thing neither my mom nor Officer Yang knew that the GEEKs' favorite hangout was a condemned observation tower in the nature preserve.

"I hope you have a good evening, Officer Yang. Thanks again," my mom said. "And don't worry—my daughter and I will have a long talk. There will be consequences for her actions."

My mouth went dry.

Officer Yang tipped his hat, climbed into his squad car, and drove off.

"Come on, young lady," Mom said. "You have some explaining to do."

I couldn't tell my mom about the treasure hunt, so I tried to launch the discussion before she could go into investigative-journalist mode. "Mom, I can explain. . . ."

"Oh, I'm sure," she said. "Let's just get home first, where we can discuss this in private."

"It was all my fault!" I burst out, as soon as we reached our apartment. "Not Elena's or Edgar's or Kevin's. So don't be mad at them. Okay?" I didn't know what the other GEEKs might be going through, but I hoped that if

I took the blame, at least they would be able to continue the treasure hunt.

Mom sat me down at the kitchen table, dropped into the chair across from me, and arched an eyebrow. "Go on."

"It's just the whole moving-from-Elmwood thing. I—"

"Don't blame your breaking into a condemned theater on the fact that we may be moving." My mom leaned forward, elbows planted on the table. "We're discussing *your* decisions here—not the decisions I have to make to do what's best for our family."

"Mom, hear me out," I said. *"Please."*

She sat back, but a vein throbbed in her neck and her fingers drummed the tabletop.

It had been over an hour since Officer Yang had responded to the silent alarm we had tripped in the theater and caught me and the other GEEKs in the auditorium. I'd had plenty of time to come up with an excuse for why we'd been there. I hated lying to my mom, but I had no choice. Too much hinged on the GEEKs' success, and there was too much risk if the town found out about our treasure hunt.

So I started with the truth and built my lie from there: "You see, Mom, all I've been able to think about lately is moving. The theater is a place I've heard stories about and seen the outside of my whole life, but I'd never seen the *inside*." I didn't have to fake the tears in my eyes. "I just wanted to get a glimpse of it before I'm forced to leave Elmwood forever."

Sauce nuzzled my knees under the table.

The vein in my mom's neck stopped throbbing. She reached across the table and took my hands. "Oh, Bean, I know this is tough. I know the thought of moving is stressful and doesn't seem fair. But that doesn't excuse poor decisions. That doesn't mean you can go around ignoring what's safe and right."

I wanted so badly to tell my mom that what was *right* was the GEEKs' search for the Van Houten fortune, but I shoved the urge aside. *Not yet,* I told myself. *Now isn't the time.*

Mom gave my hands a gentle squeeze. "You understand that trespassing was a bad decision, don't you?"

I nodded. "I know."

"I need you making *good* decisions."

"I know, Mom. I'm super sorry." My voice sounded as brittle as old newsprint. I really hoped Maxine's remaining clues only required us to visit easy-to-reach, legal places. "What's my punishment?"

Mom let go of my hands and rubbed her eyes. She seemed more tired now than angry. "Two weeks," she said. "No television."

I pushed down a smile. *No television? That's it?* I'd been braced for "No going out with your friends" or "No cell phone" or "No more journalistic assignments for the newspaper." A couple of weeks of TV time wouldn't be missed. Especially since I had a lost fortune to find.

I was more than willing to oblige when Mom said, "Now how about you go to your room and think about what you did."

As soon as I closed my door, I flopped onto my bed and checked my phone. In a figurative sense, I had about a gazillion texts from the other GEEKs. In the journalistic, literal sense, it was actually only fifty-seven.

I'd obviously been the last one to finish getting lectured, but I discovered I wasn't the only one who'd gotten pretty lucky with my punishment.

Kevin's parents were so confused by the idea of their straight-A, always-well-behaved son doing something wrong that they didn't even know *how* to punish him. Edgar got assigned early-morning milking and feeding duty for a month, but that meant he was still available to help find the fortune during the afternoons and evenings. Only Elena really got a rotten deal—her dad said the science program was off, and no amount of her begging had been able to convince him to change his mind. Along with six crying faces, she texted:

I can't believe I won't get to see the particle accelerator

"Poor Elena," I murmured. She had wanted that science program for so long, and I felt terrible that I'd played a role in getting her busted.

But Elena was never one to stay down for too long. A few minutes later, she sent another text:

did a quick search for "Elmwood" and "gingko" and came up with some pictures some photographer took. Of a gingko grove in preserve PLANTED BY MAXINE!!! go tomorrow after school?!

The rest of us responded immediately:

YES!!!!

Sunday, September 19

Observations & COGITATIONS

(Good Things About Moving)

— Mom would have a job
  ⤳ THE JOB WOULDN'T BE WITH A NEWSPAPER, SO I WOULDN'T GET TO HELP WRITE ARTICLES ANYMORE

— Spend more time with Mom's cousin Frankie
  ⤳ I REALLY LIKE FRANKIE
  ⤳ WHAT ABOUT <u>MUFFET</u>, FRANKIE'S ANKLE-BITING CAT FROM HELL???

— ~~Go to Red Sox game~~
  ⤳ I DON'T EVEN LIKE BASEBALL

— ~~Meet new people and make new friends~~
  ⤳ GEEKs RULE!!!!

— Lots of museums
  ⤳ I CAN VISIT MUSEUMS WITHOUT HAVING TO LIVE BY THEM

— ~~Get to experience life in a big city~~
  ⤳ YOU CAN'T GET MRS. DUPREE'S APPLE PIES IN BOSTON
  ⤳ I GIVE UP. THERE'S NOTHING ACTUALLY GOOD ABOUT MOVING!!!!

21

"Where's Kevin?" I asked after school on Monday, scanning Van Houten Park. "He didn't go to the Lookout, did he? He knew to come to the gazebo, right?"

"He knew," Edgar said. "I reminded him at the end of social studies."

But Kevin had raced off as soon as the bell had rung.

"We can't wait forever." Elena bounced from foot to foot. She glanced nervously toward the police station, even though we were only in the park and not doing anything remotely illegal. Yet. "We should go."

I didn't want to leave Kevin behind, especially after everything that had happened the day before, but maybe Elena was right. A blustery wind rustled through the trees, bringing gray clouds with it. Sauce circled my feet like he often did before a storm. September weather in New Hampshire can turn in a hurry, and we had a clue to solve.

We heard Kevin before we saw him.

"Kevin Robinson for sixth-grade class president! Come to the farmers market on Saturday to learn what I can do for middle schoolers and for *all* citizens of Elmwood! Spread the word! And encourage the sixth graders in your life to vote Robinson!"

We turned. Kevin had cornered old Ms. Lavoie by the statue in the center of the park and was pressing a flyer into her hands.

Ms. Lavoie took the flyer and patted Kevin's shoulder. We were too far away to hear what she said, but Kevin beamed and handed her an extra stack of flyers. Maybe if ninety-something-year-old ladies received the right to vote in sixth-grade class elections, Kevin's campaign had a chance.

He was still smiling when he got to the gazebo.

"Finally!" Elena huffed.

"Sorry." Kevin straightened his stack of remaining flyers. "Saturday will be here before you know it. I couldn't pass up a chance to spread the word about my speech. Ms. Lavoie even took extra copies of my announcement to hand out at her bridge club!"

"Seriously, Kev? We have a fortune to find. Remember?"

"So treasure hunt today, and then you guys help pass out flyers tomorrow?"

Elena gave a frustrated tug at her braid. "Kev, you've got to be kidding! We—"

"Sure, Kevin," I said, cutting Elena off before she went nuts. "Maybe we can help tomorrow. For now, can we get going? It looks like it might rain."

The other GEEKs all looked up at the thickening clouds.

"Yeah, let's go," Edgar said.

"I couldn't tell by the pictures exactly where the gingko grove is," Elena said, "but we have to start somewhere. Let's start at the Lookout and work our way south."

The four of us headed for the preserve, though we couldn't move too quickly since Elena was still limping from the previous day's theater-break-in ankle twist. As we went, Sauce wound his way in and out and around us, tail wagging.

The first grumble of thunder came when we reached the Lookout. Sauce whined and tucked his tail between his legs.

A few seconds later, a fat drop of rain found its way through the trees and splattered against my cheek. The smack of more drops sounded against the leaves overhead. Then, faster than a finger snap, the rain became a roar.

"My flyers!" Kevin yelled, tugging his T-shirt over the stack and holding it close to his chest. "We should go home!"

Which I thought was pretty rich, seeing as how it was Kevin's fault we'd had to wait so long to get to the grove and gotten caught in the rain in the first place.

Edgar pointed. "Van Houten Manor's way closer. Max will let us in!"

A burst of lightning lit our faces like the photographer's flash on school picture day. The boom of thunder came immediately afterward. There was no need to vote. We took off, Sauce leading the way.

22

Nobody answered when Kevin knocked. We huddled on the porch as water poured over clogged gutters. Water dripped down our faces, and our shoes were splattered with mud.

Edgar pressed his face against a window. "Max must've gotten the electricity turned back on. There's a light in there."

Elena banged on the door. "Hello? Max?"

I thought I might have heard someone talking inside, but it was hard to tell over the noise of the wind and the rain.

"I don't know about you GEEKs," Elena said, "but I'm getting cold. We can ask permission to come in once we're inside."

Kevin threw his arms up. (Edgar had rehomed

Kevin's flyers in his backpack.) "That doesn't even make sense!"

"That's 'cause we're not inside yet." Elena twisted the doorknob and pushed.

When the door swung open, there was no doubt I'd heard Max. His raised voice spilled down the hall from the kitchen: "I'm doing my best to play my part here. But it's not yours to find!"

Huh? Who was Max talking to?

The other GEEKs were as wide-eyed as I felt. We slipped out of our muddy shoes and headed for the kitchen.

"Please, just keep your distance," Max said to someone, his voice cracking. "I can't tell you anything more!"

We stepped through the doorway right as Max slapped his phone down onto the kitchen counter. He buried his face in his hands, his back to us. His shoulders were hunched and trembling.

That's when Sauce decided he didn't like wet fur. He shook himself, water spraying everywhere, his toenails clicking on the wooden floorboards.

Max spun, fists raised. "What the—"

"It's just us, Max!" I took a step back.

Max's face relaxed. He lowered his fists and put one hand over his heart. "Nearly gave me a heart attack," he said. "What are you kids doing here?"

I started to explain how the rainstorm came right as

154

we'd been going to search for the next clue, but Kevin cut me off.

"Who was that on the phone?" he asked, arms crossed.

"The phone?" Max put a hand back to steady himself on the counter. "Oh, yes . . . well . . ." He stared at the floor. "I suppose I owe you kids the truth."

What was going on here?

Max kept his eyes on the floor. "I'm afraid Aunt Alice must have shared the first clue with someone. She probably got desperate to find the treasure and decided to hire help." He picked up his phone, held it up like he was doing kindergarten show-and-tell. "All I know is that I've started getting strange phone calls."

"What kind of strange calls?" Kevin prodded.

I wasn't sure why Kevin was giving Max the third degree. Max didn't seem to mind Kevin's interrogation, though.

"First someone called the house, asking for Alice. When I informed the caller she'd died, I made the mistake of giving him my phone number. He started calling me, threatening me, demanding information." Max swallowed and slid his phone into his pocket. "I'm afraid he's looking for the treasure too. Fortunately, he's way behind. He was still asking questions about the cemetery."

"Have you met him?" Elena asked.

"Do you know who it is?" Edgar added.

"No, we've only talked on the phone." Max reached down and rubbed Sauce behind the ears. "I've been trying to throw him off."

"Yesterday, I saw a guy in a Yankees hat by the theater," I said, quickly explaining about the man in the baseball cap. "It seemed like he was watching us. Could he be the person calling you?"

Max gave a defeated shrug. "It could be anyone." He stopped petting Sauce and met our eyes for the first time. "Fortunately, I don't think he knows about you kids." Max scrubbed his hands across his face. "You should still be careful, though. This makes it that much more important not to share information with anybody."

"But if there's someone else looking for the treasure, wouldn't it be safest to at least tell Elena's dad?" Kevin asked. "If you're being harassed, shouldn't the police know?"

"No!" Max pressed his palms toward us. He took a deep breath. "Listen, Kevin, if we tell anyone about the clues and treasure, it will be impossible to contain the secret. Imagine every member of this town, all hunting down the treasure, all wanting it for themselves. It would tear this town apart. All we have to do is keep things under wraps a little longer and be the first ones to find the treasure. And find it quickly."

Kevin chewed the inside of his cheek. "If you say so . . ."

"Anyway," Max said, "you kids said you were in the preserve following a new clue." He shook off his earlier worry and spread his arms wide, mustering a smile. "What have my brilliant partners uncovered now?"

Elena, Edgar, and I took turns telling Max all about our discovery in Maxine's old office and how we'd uncovered the gingko-leaf clue in the theater. Kevin stayed unusually quiet through the whole explanation, even when we told about his brave climb to the theater's spotlight.

Finally, I showed Max the gingko leaf. "We figure we're looking for a specific gingko tree, and Elena learned there's a gingko grove in the preserve. We just have to find it."

Max's eyes sparkled, and he rubbed his hands together. "For once, I think I may be of some assistance. Follow me!"

Max led us up some stairs, down a long hall, and to a section of the house we'd never been to before.

"Aunt Alice's bedroom!" he announced, pushing on a door, which swung inward on squeaky hinges.

The bedroom was even more of a wreck than the rest of the house. Plaster was peeling from the ceiling and walls, revealing the wooden slats underneath.

Black soot colored the face of a stone fireplace. Empty cat-food cans littered the floor, and a birdcage with a light bulb inside dangled over a brass-framed bed covered by a stained and faded quilt. A staggering blend of sweat, rot, and cat pee thickened the air in a toxic perfume.

None of it mattered.

That's because of what hung on the wall *behind* the birdcage—an old, yellowing map of the Van Houten Nature Conservatory. We quickly huddled around the map, studying and hoping. My eyes scanned over the duck pond, the butterfly garden, the hardwood forest that was hemmed in on one side by the White Bend River. The longer I looked, the sadder I was. I thought of our crumbling Lookout. Much as we loved it, I couldn't help but imagine the way the preserve must have once been. Filled with laughing kids and kites and picnickers. The way it *should* have still been.

Until . . .

"There it is!" Edgar pointed.

In the preserve's southwest corner, the gingko grove sat tucked into an elbow of White Bend River.

The rain, which had pounded against the roof of Van Houten Manor a few minutes earlier, had quieted to a soft pitter-patter.

"Let's roll," Elena said. "A little rain won't melt us. We've gotta do the triple-G—Go Get the Gingko!"

"Wonderful," Max said. "I'll join you, if it's all right."

"Wait." Kevin held up his phone. "My parents already texted me. They want me home for dinner."

"Go," Elena said. "We can handle it."

"But . . ." Kevin paused and sighed. "I'm coming. You'll probably need me to figure out the next clue. But let's make it quick."

Sauce decided he would lead the way, even though it wasn't like he could read the map. He barreled out of the house and down the hill toward the preserve. The rest of us hurried after him, though Elena had a hard time keeping up because of her sore ankle.

"Sauce, hold on!" I called, already out of breath as I plunged down the hill.

I was shocked when he actually skidded to a halt. He snuffled the ground by the trailhead, tail wagging.

When I caught up and saw what lay smashed in the mud, I realized Sauce hadn't stopped because of my command. He'd only stopped because he can't resist when something stinks.

23

Two cigarette butts had been trampled along the edge of the trail. With all the rain, it was impossible to tell how long they'd been there, but I hadn't noticed them earlier.

"Yankees Man," I said. "He smoked." I pushed the muddy cigarette butts around with the toe of my sneaker. "Do you think he's following us?"

"If he is," Edgar said, "that means he must know about the fortune *and* about us helping Max."

Max's face looked a little pale, but the sky was still overcast, so it may have been a trick of the light. "People cut through the preserve once in a while," he said. "I see them from the house. Let's hope it's just someone taking a shortcut." He looked over his shoulders, then peered into the woods. "But we should be careful."

"No loud voices," Kevin ordered. "If someone's in the woods listening, we don't want them to know what we're doing."

"Don't worry, Kev. We know," Elena said. "Let's just go."

So we did.

We took the trail past the Lookout, winding around until we could hear the river through the trees. A muddy track that must once have been some kind of road ran parallel to the river, and all we had to do was follow it. Which was easier said than done, since it was completely overgrown. Max insisted on going first, to clear the path for the rest of us. Still, briars scratched at our ankles as we walked. We'd been stomping through the weeds for ten minutes when we rounded a curve in the trail and Elena gasped and pointed.

A dozen gingko trees were planted ahead in a large circle, though what had once been a clearing in the middle of the trees was now a tangled mess of weeds and undergrowth. The trees were at least fifty feet high and beginning to show their fall colors, bright yellow bands forming on the ends of the leaves.

We walked around, examining each tree. Sauce helped by snuffling around the trunks. But there was nothing.

"Now what?" Edgar asked. "Do we have to climb a dozen different trees and hope we find something?"

"I recognized the saying from the back of the gingko leaf," Kevin said in a low voice. "I think Pastor Fernlaw quoted it from the Bible in one of his Sunday sermons."

"So what's it mean?" Elena asked.

Kevin grimaced. "I don't pay *that* much attention in church."

Max pulled out his phone and tried to Google it, but he couldn't get a signal. Cell reception stinks in the nature preserve.

"Read the clue again, Gina," Edgar said.

I pulled out the wooden gingko leaf and read the words carved into its back: " 'She is like a tree planted by streams of water that yields its fruit in season and its leaf does not wither.' "

Elena studied one of the nearby trees. "What about the *she* and *fruit* in the verse? Before my abuela moved in with us, she lived in an apartment with a gingko tree nearby. Every year, the tree's fruity seeds would drop and stink up the whole neighborhood. It smelled like someone had puked on the sidewalk!"

"But what do stinky seeds have to do with *she*?" Edgar asked.

"That's the thing," Elena said. "There are guy and girl gingko trees, and only the *female* trees have the fruit."

I grinned and pointed. "You mean like that?"

Sauce—my stink-loving dog—was circling around

and around one of the gingko trees, his ears dragging, his nose to the ground.

"Sauce for the win!" Edgar said. "Guess someone should start climbing."

"I'll do—" I started to say. But Elena was already reaching for the lowest branch.

"Not a chance," Kevin said. "I'll do it. You have a twisted ankle. Remember?"

"I can—" I tried again. I saw Max's eyes flicker in my direction.

"Well, Kev," Elena said, "you nearly peed your pants climbing on the catwalk. *Remember?*"

Max put a hand on Kevin's and Elena's shoulders. "Come on. You kids are a team." He looked at Elena. "Kevin's right, though—you shouldn't climb with an injured ankle."

"But—"

"And, Kevin"—Max turned to him—"Elena's also right. It sounds like you had some trouble with heights in the theater."

"But—"

"Can you do it, Gina?" Max turned to me. "I can give you a boost."

Warmth flooded my face. Max knew I wanted to do it, and he trusted *me* to get the job done! "Sure," I said. "I can climb."

Before Kevin or Elena could argue, Max laced his

fingers together down by his knees. I boosted off his hands and hauled myself into the gingko tree.

As a journalist, I'd never had to climb a tree to get a scoop. But now I pulled myself up branch by branch, running my hands over the rough trunk, peeking over and under and around each limb, searching for anything out of place. About twenty feet up, I spotted something. I nearly didn't see the box—it was so rusty it blended in with the brown of the trunk—but the sharp angle of a protruding corner gave it away.

"A box!" I called to my friends. "There's a metal box padlocked to the trunk with a combination lock!"

Everyone started yelling at once: "Woo-hoo! We found it!" and "Open it!" and "Hurry up! I wanna see!"

"Well done, Gina!" Max called. "Be careful up there."

"Try the numbers carved into the back of the gingko leaf," Kevin called, his mind quickly spinning through the math. "Most combination locks use three different numbers with none more than two digits long. Just like our lockers at school. The digits one-one-four-five-six can only be broken apart three different ways. You can start by trying eleven, forty-five, six."

FACT #1: Kevin was right—using the digits from the back of the wooden gingko leaf, there were three possible combinations for the lock.

164

FACT #2: I tried all three combinations before I finally landed on the right one.

FACT #3: When the lock popped free and I opened the box, I found a single sheet of paper folded inside.

Extreme congratulations!

You're halfway through my test.

Use smarts, hard work, and wisdom.

Do you know Elmwood best?

Within a shadow of five points,

Gaze up and you will see—

The big bear kisses Jupiter

By my exalted key.

I hurried down the tree and showed the clue to the others.

"What do you think the 'shadow of five points' thing means?" Elena asked.

"And what about 'the big bear kisses Jupiter'?" Edgar said.

"Hold on." Kevin put a finger to his lips. "We shouldn't talk about it here. We don't know who may be listening."

"We're in the middle of the woods," Elena protested.

"We're getting too close," Kevin whispered. "We can't be too safe."

"Come back to the manor," Max said. "We can talk about it there."

"Good idea," I said. "We can—"

"No," Kevin said. "I need to get home, remember? Besides, it's getting late. Let's head home and share our theories tomorrow."

I wanted to argue, to keep searching, to follow our new lead to its conclusion. I saw a crestfallen look cross Max's face too. But Edgar piped up to say he had chores at the farm, and even Elena said she couldn't afford to get in any more trouble, so we all said our goodbyes.

Since Edgar and I were going the same direction, he came with me and Sauce as we followed the river east. We didn't need to split up until we popped from the preserve by the Elmgrove Bridge on White Bend Road.

"Say hi to Ollie for me," I told Edgar.

He grinned. "Best cow in the world!"

That's when my cell signal returned. My phone and Edgar's pinged simultaneously. It was a message to the GEEKs from Kevin. Seven simple, one-syllable words that made my stomach tighten:

I'm not sure we should trust Max.

Observations & COGITATIONS

(Strange Man Spotted Near the Theater)

— Yankees cap

⤳ A YANKEES FAN IN ELMWOOD???
SUSPICIOUS!!!

— Stringy gray hair

⤳ I ONLY SAW THE HAIR STICKING FROM
UNDER THE SIDES OF HIS CAP. COULD HE
BE GOING BALD?

— Smokes cigarettes

⤳ DOESN'T HE CARE ABOUT THE RISK OF
LUNG CANCER?

⤳ ARE HIS CIGARETTES THE SAME BRAND
SAUCE FOUND NEAR VAN HOUTEN MANOR?

— Looked away every time I glanced toward him from
outside the theater

⤳ DOUBLE SUSPICIOUS!!!

24

Mom sat slumped over some paperwork in the newspaper office when Sauce and I got home. "Hey, Bean," she said, pushing back from her desk. "I've had a long day. Want to watch a few episodes of *Gilmore Girls* tonight?"

Gilmore Girls was our comfort show, but I was suspicious. I was supposedly grounded from TV for two weeks. Had Mom already forgotten my punishment? Or was she trying to distract me, hoping to talk more about moving? No way was I risking another discussion about Boston and new jobs and Cousin Frankie. Plus, I really needed to talk to Kevin about his text.

"Didn't you ground me from TV?" I asked, probably becoming the first sixth grader in history to intentionally remind her mother about a punishment. "Plus, I need to work on some, uh . . . school stuff."

Mom sighed. "You're right. I'd already forgotten your no-TV punishment. Thanks for being so honest."

Of course, I didn't actually feel all that honest as I hustled to my room, where I had absolutely no school-work to do (GEEKs tend to finish their homework by four p.m.) but a very important phone call to make. I sat on the edge of my bed and dialed.

Kevin answered on the first ring. "Hello?"

"What do you mean we can't trust Max?"

"Yes, Gina, I'm fine. Thanks for asking," Kevin said sarcastically.

"Sorry . . . but seriously, what do you mean?"

"I'm just getting a weird vibe from the guy," Kevin said.

"A weird vibe? That's it?"

"It's hard to explain." I could practically hear the eye roll in Kevin's voice.

I rolled my eyes right back.

"Don't you think you might be getting paranoid?" I asked. "Max is the one who told us about the treasure in the first place. All he's done is help us."

"But weren't you paying attention when he told us about the phone call? He didn't meet our eyes. You're the journalist, Gina. If a source doesn't meet your eyes, what's that tell you?"

I knew lack of eye contact could be a classic clue that someone was lying. But it wasn't like that was the *only* possibility. "He was probably embarrassed because he'd been keeping the phone calls secret, and we caught him," I finally said. "Plus, he was petting Sauce. It's not weird to look at a dog while you're petting it."

"Okay," Kevin said, "then why didn't he tell us about the phone calls in the first place?"

I flopped onto my back and stared at the ceiling. "Max is being harassed. It's probably worse than he's letting on. He wants to shield us. Protect us."

"Or maybe he's got something to hide."

I couldn't believe we were even having this conversation! I was the journalist. I was the one who spent every day observing people and writing down my thoughts while Kevin was busy with chess club and class elections. "We can trust him, Kevin. I feel it."

"So now *you're* the one with the vibes?" Kevin asked. "You always want facts, Gina, and the facts show that Maxine was nice but the rest of the family was a bunch of jerks. So how do we know Max isn't a jerk too? What do we even know about him?"

"He wants to save our town, Kevin."

"You mean he wants our help to find a lot of money."

"Money that's going to save Elmwood!" I cried in frustration.

The future of the town was at stake. And if we didn't

find this treasure, and fast, Mom and I would be packing our things for Boston. Kevin had picked the worst possible moment to go spouting conspiracy theories about Max, and suddenly I thought I knew why. "You know what, Kevin? I think you're jealous."

Kevin snorted. "Of what?"

"Since the beginning, Max has treated me like the leader. He was thankful to *me* for getting him out of that vault. He trusted *me* with Maxine's letter. He helped *me* climb the tree in the gingko grove to get the last clue. You obviously don't like it. It seems like you care more about being elected class president than about saving our town!"

"That's—you—you're—" Kevin stammered. "You're being naïve, Gina."

My mom picked that moment to knock on my door. "Gina Bean, I have a study treat for you."

"I've gotta go, Kevin," I said.

And I hung up.

Still, I heard Kevin's voice echoing in my head. I might have been right about Kevin, but he was right about me, too.

A reporter had to trust her instincts, and my instincts told me Max was trying to help us. But Kevin and I had been friends for years. I had only known Max for days. How could I trust him over Kevin unless I had the facts?

Mom opened my door, carrying a plate of blondies. Sauce trailed in after her. "Not to ruin your dinner later, but . . . I needed a break this afternoon," she said. "So I baked."

"Your break, my benefit." I sat up and forced a smile, hoping Mom wouldn't notice there was absolutely no schoolwork in sight. I plucked a blondie from the plate and took a huge bite. The chopped walnuts and white chocolate chips were almost enough to cheer me up for real.

Mom settled in next to me on my bed.

"Mom," I said, blondie crumbs dropping from my mouth, "how can you prove someone is telling the truth? You know, like when you're investigating a story—how do you know to trust a source?"

Sauce wriggled onto the bed between us, and Mom scratched his ears. "You can't ever really be a hundred percent sure, but a good journalist always checks her facts. Whatever stories or information a source tells me, I work to verify every part I can. If someone has lied about one thing, chances are they've lied about more. If they've told the truth about all the things I can fact-check . . . well, I can probably trust them." Mom handed me another blondie. "Why the interest in trustworthy sources? Getting ready to break a big story?"

I smirked. "You think I'm going to let you steal my scoop? Nice try, Mom."

Mom ruffled my hair. "I've trained you too well!"

Sauce barked, as if he agreed. But it was probably just his way of saying he wanted a blondie.

The three of us—me, Mom, and Sauce—hung out in my bedroom, eating blondies and talking (or, in Sauce's case, snoring), and I managed to keep the conversation away from anything to do with Boston. Despite everything else I had to think and worry about, hanging out with my mom was actually kind of nice.

When only a few stray crumbs were left on the plate, Mom said, "I suppose this study break has gone longer than I'd intended." She stood. "I'll let you get back to it."

"Okay," I said. I rubbed my stomach. "And thanks. The blondies were delicious."

Mom blew me a kiss, gently pulling my door shut as she left my room.

As soon as the latch clicked, I counted to ten. Then I fired up my laptop, got online, and Googled *Max Van Houten*.

I was a journalist—a *good* one. It was time to fact-check.

25

At school on Tuesday, I waited all day to tell Kevin what I'd found out about Max the night before. But Kevin spent lunchtime in the library with the chess club, and we had our French Revolution test in Mr. Singh's class, so there was no time to talk.

After school, the GEEKs decided together to skip the Lookout. The memory of those cigarette butts was still fresh in our minds. Instead, we headed downtown, though Elena insisted we sit on the back side of the gazebo, out of sight of the police station.

Kevin didn't look my way as we rolled our bikes through the grass, and I could tell he was still upset about what I'd said last night. I wondered if I had been too harsh. . . .

As we leaned our bikes against the gazebo, I said, "Hey, guys, after Kevin's text yesterday, I—"

"I have more to say about that," Kevin said. "Did you hear what Max said on the phone? 'I'm doing my best to play my part'? How do we know he's actually Max? What if he's an actor, like Edgar?"

I groaned. "Max isn't an actor, Kevin. The only part he's playing is his part in saving Elmwood."

"How do you know?"

"I decided you were right," I said. Kevin finally looked my way, surprised. "We needed more facts. So I Googled Max last night. I fact-checked. Max Van Houten definitely exists."

"Just because he exists, that doesn't mean the guy in the manor is actually Max."

"I found some mentions of him online in articles about the Van Houten family, but there's never any pictures of him. There's not much else because he's kept a super-low profile and doesn't use social media, probably because he's sick of being in the spotlight as a Van Houten. But . . ." I pulled a printout from my backpack and showed it to the other GEEKs. "I found this."

Elena, Edgar, and Kevin studied the photo, which had been posted to the Facebook page of a school called Grantwood Preparatory by someone named Chip Mac-Dougal. It appeared to be from an old yearbook. Three teenage boys—two kneeling and one more standing in the middle behind them—pointed proudly at a foot-tall robot that had two oversized, clawlike hands. The caption read: *Old buddies! Max Van Houten, James Hatcher, and me with CHOMPER, the robot we built for the Inter-Prep Battlebots Showdown. The good old days!*

"That's definitely a younger Max." Edgar pointed at the boy on the left.

"So . . . *fact*," I said, raising one finger, trying not to sound too triumphant.

Elena pointed to the school's name. "And he went to Grantwood Prep, like he told us."

"So . . . fact again." I raised a second finger. "Which means . . . fact. Max has been telling us the truth."

Kevin sighed heavily, like he had a newspaper printing press mashing against his chest. "Fine, you fact-checked. There's just something about the guy. . . ."

"I know you don't like him," I said gently. "But he's offered us our only shot at saving Elmwood. Are we going to waste it?"

Kevin frowned. "I'm not sure it's our *only* chance, but you made your point. Can we get on with the clue?"

Some of the tightness I'd felt in my chest melted away. Sure, Kevin had only reluctantly accepted the facts about Max. But it was a start. At least it felt like the GEEKs were on the same team again.

As I pulled out the clue we'd found in the gingko grove, Sophina sauntered past on her way to the bakery. "Hey, it's the four GEEKs!" she said. "Or are you the four delinquents now? You know—after your little Sunday adventure with the Elmwood police."

Elena narrowed her eyes. "How do you even know about that?"

Sophina kept walking. "News spreads fast in a small town, GEEKs. Wonder how this will affect your election chances, Kevin?"

She tilted her head back in a laugh as she sauntered off.

Elena tugged at her braid. "Ooh, I really can't stand that girl. . . ."

"That makes two of us," grumbled Kevin. "I can't let her become class president."

"Let's worry about the *treasure*," I said. I waved the clue over my head, which finally seemed to get everyone's attention.

We decided to focus on the clue's second half, which was definitely the most confusing:

Within a shadow of five points,

Gaze up and you will see—

The big bear kisses Jupiter

By my exalted key.

We shared all sorts of ideas, like "Maybe the big bear is in a circus!" and "My dad shaves every morning, but by dinnertime his beard's growing back and he calls it his 'five o'clock shadow.' Could that have something to do with 'a shadow of five points'?"

It was Kevin who finally came up with something that almost made sense: "Bamboozleland had a ride called the Shooting Star, didn't it? Couldn't that have a five-pointed shadow? And maybe there were other rides, like Jupiter and Big Bear."

"It's possible," Edgar said. "I don't remember. That place closed down when we were still in kindergarten."

I thought of Bamboozleland, which Maxine had built at the height of the Bamboozler's popularity. The amusement park had faded, just like its namesake toy, until it had finally closed for good about six years ago. "That's good, Kev. But how would we even get in?" I asked. "The fence around Bamboozleland is massive. Too tall even for Elena."

No one said anything for a minute. It was Edgar who broke the silence.

"If we can't go over, we could go under," he said.

Elena's eyes lit up. "Dig a *tunnel*? I am so in."

"No, I mean, we could cut a hole in the wire," Edgar said. "I helped my dad take down an old barbed-wire fence on our farm last year, and we used a pair of bolt cutters. I bet they're still in his toolshed."

"Excellent," said Elena, rubbing her hands together. Kevin, on the other hand, looked wary.

"Can you go get them now?" I asked.

Edgar bit his lip. "My dad wouldn't like me using them," he said. "But . . . he *would* want what's best for the farm. And that's getting the next clue."

"The farm forces a detour, so we've got no time to lose," said Elena. "Let's go!"

Bamboozleland was on Scrubstone Lane, past the high school and the toy factory. The park wasn't that large, but it used to be nice—a place where families could go for summertime fun, where school groups could visit after touring Van Houten Toys. Now it was just creepy.

We cycled around to the back of the park, and Edgar got to work. One by one, he cut the links of the fence in an L shape. Then he pulled it back like a curtain and ushered us through. Elena hesitated, still eyeing the bolt cutters. I had a feeling that they already had a part to play in a future prank she was planning.

"Do you think I might be able to borrow . . . ," she started, in her sweetest voice.

Edgar shook his head sternly. Elena sighed, then ducked through the fence. I followed, with Kevin close on my heels and Edgar squeezing through last.

The ground was covered in weeds, trash, and decomposing leaves. Many of the rides had been torn out once Bamboozleland closed, and what was left included the skeletal remains of a Ferris wheel and an old wooden roller coaster that poked into the sky like the bones of some massive extinct beast. Miniature train tracks, where a kid-sized train once ran, wove through the park. All the paths were spokes in a wheel, leading to the park's center, where a worn-out carousel huddled like a frightened rabbit.

Edgar located a sign with a faded map of the park. There were no Jupiter or Big Bear rides, so we headed for the Shooting Star. Or at least for what *should* have been the Shooting Star. All we found were a couple of rusted steel plates still bolted to the ground.

"It's *gone*. . . ." I blinked, my eyes burning.

Kevin moaned. "We're ruined. Done. Maxine didn't know the amusement park would close. She didn't know the Shooting Star would get bulldozed, maybe with her clue inside it!"

For once, even Elena didn't crack a joke. "Yeah," she said. "And if we don't get that treasure . . . what if downtown Elmwood looks like this in a few years? The toy factory . . . the Maple Leaf . . . the school all just empty shells."

Edgar gave a little whimper. "The school?"

But Elena's comment jolted my brain. "Wait," I said.

"Back up." My heartbeat quickened. "We could be closer to the solution than we thought."

"How?" Kevin frowned. "There's no more Shooting Star, Gina."

"Sure, the clue could have meant the Shooting Star, because a star has five points." I pretended to draw a star in the air in front of me. Then I air-erased it, bent down, and plucked a half-rotted leaf from the ground, waving it at my friends. "But so does a maple leaf."

26

Four facts convinced the other GEEKs to meet me back downtown at six o'clock that evening:

FACT #1: Sunset was going to be at 6:38 p.m.

FACT #2: A maple leaf can have three, five, or seven lobes.

FACT #3: The Maple Leaf Diner has a sign on the roof that's shaped like an oversized, five-lobed maple leaf—a leaf with five different points.

FACT #4: The sign faces east, so as the sun set, it would cast a five-pointed shadow in front of the diner.

I talked Mom into an early dinner, telling her that Kevin and I had a social studies project to work on. As soon we finished washing the dishes, I said, "I'm going to go meet Kevin now. That okay?"

"Of course, Bean." Mom waved me off with a dish towel. "I'm thankful you kids are so proactive with your schoolwork. Don't forget your helmet."

"Sure thing." I grabbed my helmet and backpack. "See you later."

I left Sauce snoring on his pile of old newspapers and shot out the door.

As I pedaled into town, I tried not to think about how easily I'd just lied to my mom. Again. We'd always been honest with each other, but now everything seemed different. Mom was hiding her FINAL NOTICE paper from me. I was hiding the GEEKs' treasure hunt from her.

We just need to find the fortune, I told myself. *If we solve the puzzle, we save Elmwood. Then it will all be worth it.*

I repeated that over and over in my head for the entire ride into town, hoping it would eventually feel true. Hoping I'd start to feel more like an undercover journalist, using justifiable deceit to track down a story, and less like just another kid lying to her mom.

As I coasted to a stop in front of the Maple Leaf, the other GEEKs were also arriving. Evening shadows already crept over the town, and the sun crawled toward the horizon in the west while the moon climbed upward in the east. Even from the sidewalk, the delicious smells of the Maple Leaf hung in the air, warm and familiar.

"Watch the shadow, everybody," Kevin said.

"Duh," Elena replied.

I just pulled the pencil from my hair and prepared to take notes.

For nearly forty minutes we watched the Maple Leaf's five-pointed shadow shift along the ground, moving from the sidewalk to the road. We paid attention to where the lobes of the leaf seemed to point (nowhere useful). And we noted everything the shadow covered (cracked cement and asphalt).

When the sun had completely disappeared, leaving only a faint orange glow in the sky, Kevin sagged to the sidewalk. "It's another five-pointed failure!"

Elena kicked at a pebble on the sidewalk, sending it skittering into the street.

Behind us, a bell jangled. We turned. Mrs. Dupree stepped from the diner and flipped the sign on the door to CLOSED.

"Oh, good evening," she said when she saw us. She looked tired, but she flashed us a small smile. "You weren't wanting into the diner were you? I haven't had any evening customers, so I decided to close early."

"Don't worry, Mrs. Dupree," Edgar said. "We're just watching the sunset."

Mrs. Dupree smiled. "The diner usually makes me miss that part of nature's show." She pointed to the sky above Van Houten Park. "But at least tonight I can enjoy a nearly full moon."

As Mrs. Dupree climbed into her pickup truck, Kevin said, "The moon! Of course!" His thumbs flew across his phone.

"What is it, Kevin?" I asked.

"We all know Jupiter is a planet, but 'Big Bear' is—"

"Ursa Major!" Elena cried. "Oh, sweet Einstein! I'm a scientist. How did I miss that? Jupiter and Big Bear—a planet and a constellation!"

"Exactly," Kevin said. "We're supposed to look at the night sky."

Elena balled both her hands into fists and let out a frustrated "Aaargh! . . . If only I had enough to get the telescope I've been saving up for. We could really use one now."

Mrs. Dupree, who was just rolling by in her truck at that moment, poked her head out the open window. "Did you say you needed a telescope?"

We all looked at one another, then back at her. "Yeah," Elena answered. "Why? Do you have one? Preferably a high-powered telescope for stargazing?"

Mrs. Dupree laughed. "Oh no. I enjoy the night sky—plenty of it to see out here, away from big cities—but

I'm afraid I don't have a telescope. But if you need to learn something about the stars, you should talk to old Bob Hensworth."

"Who's he?" My pencil hovered above my notebook, ready.

"Lives in that tiny cabin north of town, just past the dump," Mrs. Dupree answered. "It's an older place—what around Elmwood isn't? But he keeps it tip-top tidy. Bob comes to the diner the last Tuesday of every month. Big fan of my ham-and-bean dinner. Knows everything there is to know about the stars, too. If anyone in Elmwood has a telescope, it'd be old Bob Hensworth. Have to warn you, though, he's kind of crotchety. But, well . . ." Mrs. Dupree winked at us. "Not everyone can be a sweetheart like you children."

And Mrs. Dupree drove off.

Elena did a facepalm. "Maybe I didn't deserve to go to that science program after all. How could I have missed such an obvious clue about the Big Bear?"

I put a hand on Elena's shoulder. "The important thing is we're figuring it out. We're getting closer all the time."

"But how much time do we even have?" Kevin asked.

"None tonight. It's getting late." I showed the clock display on my phone. "Should we try to find Bob Hensworth's tomorrow after school?"

"I don't know," Edgar said. "You heard Mrs. Dupree—

he's crotchety. What's he going to do when a bunch of sixth graders show up at his house?"

Kevin puffed his chest out. "I'm not scared. I can talk to anyone. It's part of being a leader."

"Yeah, Kev," Elena said. "You can just give him a flyer about your speech. That should totally break the ice."

Kevin missed the sarcasm in Elena's voice. "Yes! Perfect! I'll tell Bob Hensworth about my speech on Saturday, then ask him about Ursa Major!"

Elena arched an eyebrow. "Kind of a major topic swap, don't you think?"

Kevin waved off Elena's concern. "I can pull it off."

I sure hoped Kevin was right.

Tuesday, September 21

Top ~~10~~ 4 Rides at Bamboozleland

(according to the memories of 5-year-old me)

4. FERRIS WHEEL. There probably would have been a good view of Elmwood when the ride stopped at the top. Unfortunately, I had my face buried in my mom's shoulder, too afraid to look.

3. THE PUDDLE JUMPER. I think it had something to do with spinning lily pads. I don't remember for sure. I DO remember it was a regrettable ride choice right after eating a chili dog and chips.

2. CAROUSEL. Brightly painted horses that slowly went up and down as the carousel turned, organ music piping into the park. It wasn't real exciting, but at least I wasn't scared, and it didn't make me throw up.

1. BUMP-A-SAURUS WRECKS. Bumper cars shaped like mini dinosaurs. Definitely the best ride in Bamboozleland! (At least, it was the best ride for a five-year-old too short for every other ride in the park.*)

* Since I was too short for most of the rides, Mom let me visit a bunch of game booths. I won a giant purple elephant at the Ellie-Fun-Trunk Ring Toss. I had it for years—until Sauce came into our lives and mistook my prize for a supersized doggy toy. RIP, purple elephant.

27

I only learned one thing at school on Wednesday—searching for hidden treasure makes it impossible to learn anything at school. I was totally distracted. As soon as the end-of-day bell rang, the other GEEKs and I bolted from Mr. Singh's classroom. Elena took a quick detour home for something; then we biked toward Bob Hensworth's.

We almost pedaled right past it. The cabin was just beyond the town dump, like Mrs. Dupree had said, but lay hidden behind thick trees. Fortunately, Edgar spotted the mailbox with HENSWORTH stenciled on the side.

Kevin pointed to the PRIVATE PROPERTY—KEEP OUT sign hammered to the mailbox's post. "Maybe we should—"

"Roll on, GEEKs!" Elena took off down the long, winding driveway, dust kicking up from her bike tires.

The rest of us followed her.

I spotted three more PRIVATE PROPERTY signs nailed to trees. At the end of the drive, the tiny cabin almost seemed like part of the surrounding woods. It was built from thick, weathered logs and had a dark green metal roof, which extended in the front to cover a small porch. The cabin would've looked abandoned—like so much else in Elmwood—except that the small patch of grass out front was neatly trimmed, a well-tended garden along the side held pumpkins and lettuce and other vegetables, and there was even a small greenhouse.

The cabin's door included one final PRIVATE PROPERTY sign, just in case any visitors missed the first four.

Elena jumped off her bike and headed for the porch.

"Wait!" Kevin called. He rummaged around in his backpack and pulled out a flyer. "I'm the one doing this. Remember? My speech!"

Elena rolled her eyes, but she stopped and let Kevin take the lead.

Kevin took a deep breath, stepped onto the porch, and gave two soft knocks. Nobody answered.

Elena sighed. Loudly. "Might need to knock harder than a mushy banana, Kev."

"That doesn't even—" Kevin threw up his hands. "Oh, never mind." He gave two more knocks on the door, this time a little louder.

"Go away!" a voice growled from inside. "I don't want to buy any!"

Kevin jumped back and nearly fell off the porch.

The flyer about his Saturday speech trembled in his hand, but he squared his shoulders and stepped back up to the door. This time he gave three sharp raps and called, "We're not selling anything, sir!"

The stomp of feet pounded from inside. The door flew open. And that's when I learned what an angry Santa Claus would look like.

Bob Hensworth was tall and round, his white hair thick and uncombed. His bushy white beard hung halfway down the front of his red-and-black-checked flannel shirt. His equally bushy white eyebrows pinched together in an angry V.

"Why, hello, sir," Kevin said, extending his hand. "My name is—"

"Can't you read? 'Private property. Keep out.'" Bob Hensworth smacked his palm against the sign on his door. "Got the signs for a reason!"

Then Angry Santa slammed the door.

Kevin stood there, hand still out, statue-like.

"Wow, Kev," Elena said. "Very leaderly. Planning to introduce yourself to the doorknob?"

I tried not to laugh but couldn't help myself. It *was* kind of funny. Plus, laughing helped cover my

191

disappointment. If Bob Hensworth was the only way to solve the latest clue, we weren't getting any closer.

Kevin dropped his outstretched hand and trudged off the porch.

"It's okay, Kevin," Edgar said. "You tried. That's what leaders do, right?"

Which made me feel pretty rotten about laughing.

"Yeah, Kev. I was only joking. We'll figure something out." Elena reached for her bike, then froze. She stared at the greenhouse along the side of the cabin. "What the *what*? Is that an aquaponics garden?"

I studied the greenhouse a little closer. It looked like it had a few old bathtubs stacked inside.

"I can't believe it!" Elena rushed over and pressed her face against the greenhouse's glass wall, her voice rising in excitement. "He's got two tubs for fish, two for large plants, and another just for seedlings. It's a brilliant application of aquaponics principles!"

"Elena," Kevin said, "whatever it is, forget it. I don't think my parents would ignore a second call from the police."

"But I've never seen an aquaponics garden in person before, Kev. And anyone who has an aquaponics garden can't be *all* bad!"

"Didn't you notice we're not really wanted here?" Kevin said. "If we don't—"

"I told you kids to leave."

I gasped. Kevin dropped his flyer. Elena flinched, smacking her forehead into the greenhouse.

Angry Santa—Bob Hensworth—stood by the corner of his cabin, clutching a shovel like a baseball bat.

Edgar, of course, tried to exit stage left—only there was no stage, so instead he tripped backward over his bike.

"I'm—we're—we didn't—" Kevin waved the flyer about his speech like a flag of surrender. "We were just—"

"Did you design this aquaponics system?" Elena asked.

Bob Hensworth's eyebrows shifted from anger to confusion. "Oh. Well. You—you're familiar with aquaponics?"

"It's so good for the environment!" Elena said. Then she launched into some rambling speech about "a naturally organic, symbiotic system that combines aquaculture and hydroponics to promote sustainable, efficient food production."

Bob Hensworth nodded his head and started to smile, lowering his shovel and leaning it against the side of the cabin. He pointed at his greenhouse. "I designed this system myself. Would you like to see it up close?"

"Seriously?" Elena bounced up and down. "Yes, yes, yes!"

The next thing I knew, all of us GEEKs stood huddled

around a bunch of old bathtubs in Bob Hensworth's greenhouse as he talked about "plant-based filtration" and a bunch of other sciencey stuff. I know I didn't understand everything as well as Elena did, but I have to admit—it was still pretty cool.

Kevin patted one of the bathtubs. "Maybe the environmental benefits of aquaponics are something I could bring to the community's attention if I'm elected."

Bob scratched at his beard. "Aren't you a bit young for politics?"

Kevin threw his shoulders back, chest out. "I'm running for sixth-grade class president. But I want to do more than just improve our school—I want to help the entire town. I'm even making a speech on Saturday at the Elmwood Farmers Market. Well, technically I'm still writing the speech, but I'll have it done before Saturday. I'd appreciate your attendance and support."

Yeah, I know it seems like a wild transition, but— somehow—Kevin pulled it off.

Bob took the flyer Kevin offered. His mumbled reply was rumbly and rough but not unfriendly: "I might just make it. Not a big fan of crowds, but I appreciate your enthusiasm and vision for our town."

"Speaking of crowds . . . ," Kevin said. "I know there are a lot of stars crowded into the sky, even when we can't see them, and we heard you were an expert on the constellations. In fact, that's why we stopped by today."

Oof. That transition? Not so good. But Bob didn't seem to mind.

He shuffled his feet and adjusted a tube running into one of the bathtubs filled with fish. "I studied astronomy at MIT. Worked a lot of years for NASA before I moved back to Elmwood to live closer to the land."

At Bob's mention of NASA, Elena looked ready to faint. "Do you have a telescope?"

A moment later, Bob Hensworth was leading us out of his greenhouse and into his cabin.

Other than an open door that led into a small bathroom, the inside of the cabin was a single room. It had a tidy kitchen area, a neatly made bed pushed against one wall, a square table with a bench made from a split tree trunk, and a few bookcases filled with books that had titles like *The Encyclopedia of Astronomy and Astrophysics* and *Detecting Exoplanets through Radial Velocity*. But the highlight of the cabin sat in a corner near the front door—a shiny black telescope so large it looked like a cannon.

28

"Over four hundred years ago, Galileo became the first person to use a telescope to study the stars and planets." Bob patted the top of his telescope. "I often wonder what he'd think if he'd been able to roll *this* outside on a clear night."

Elena ran her finger slowly down the telescope's length. "When and where would we look to see Ursa Major kissing Jupiter?"

Bob frowned. "Well, even Einstein never figured out time travel, so you'd have to wait until next year. That astronomical event happens in the spring, not the fall."

Elena's hand dropped away from Bob's telescope. "That's the only time?"

Bob nodded. "It's the only time in this area. I have a book about the constellations around here that might have pictures of what you're asking about, and I'd be happy to lend it to you." He scanned his shelves, then shook his head. "Must be in my cellar. You kids want one more quick change of scenery?"

Kevin looked hesitant, and I got why. Not following a strange old man into a basement is, as Elena would say, chapter one of *Stranger Danger 101*. But we were here on Mrs. Dupree's recommendation, and she *wasn't* a stranger. And besides, did the normal rules really apply when you were searching for life-changing treasure? (I knew what Mom's answer to this question would be, but I ignored it.)

Kevin must have been thinking the same thing, because he followed as Bob grabbed a flashlight and took us outside to the back of the cabin. Near the ground, two wooden doors with wrought-iron hinges angled away from the cabin's stone foundation. Bob pulled them open. Worn wooden steps led into darkness. When we reached the bottom of the stairs, Bob clicked on his flashlight.

"Whoa," Edgar said, looking around. "Cool."

The ceiling was low, and Bob had to duck to avoid the thick log beams overhead. The outer walls of the cellar were stacked stones, and the floor was packed dirt. An old, earthy smell clung to the cool air. The only hints we hadn't time-traveled to the 1800s were the sealed plastic totes that lined one wall, each labeled with a hand-printed tag.

"What's through there?" Elena asked, pointing to an open doorway to the right of the stairs.

Bob swung his flashlight beam through the doorway, revealing a strange room. Plastic barrels lined the metal walls on one side. Mattresses were stacked on the other. In the middle of the room was a long wooden box.

Kevin gasped, his eyes widening. "Um—is that—a—a—"

"It's a coffin!" Elena squealed. "Inside some kind of dungeon!"

Edgar plopped down on the bottom stair. I took a step toward the doorway. "Uh—we should probably get going. . . ."

My heart thudded. Why had we let ourselves be led into the dark cellar of a crotchety old man we didn't really know? You couldn't treasure-hunt if you were six feet under. . . .

Bob gave a short laugh. "Sorry. Didn't mean to spook you. Guess I'm not too used to visitors. But it's not a coffin."

"It isn't?" I reminded myself that I should always seek facts, not rumors. Trying to behave more like a cool, calm journalist, I inched forward and asked, "What is it, then?"

"You see," Bob said, checking the labels on the plastic totes as he talked, "this cabin has been in my family for generations. Built by hand by my great-great-great-grandfather. I grew up here myself."

"So your parents lived here too?" Elena asked.

Bob nodded. "And in the sixties, during the Cold War, lots of people were scared of nuclear war. So my father built a fallout shelter, with enough room for us and anyone else in town who didn't have anywhere to go." He shone his flashlight around the cabin's stone foundation, then focused it back on the room. "The barrels are full of water. Or they were. The box is full of flashlights and matches, things like that. Though the Cold War ended a long time ago, I keep this place around as a reminder that science is great, but it can be used to destroy. I'd rather we use it to bring people together."

"I didn't know anyone here was scared enough back then to build fallout shelters," Kevin said with quiet awe in his voice. "Elmwood has always felt so safe to me."

"It was a scary time for everyone," Bob said, his reverent tone matching Kevin's. "Thankfully, what my father most feared never came to pass. But neither did world peace. We're still a long way off from that. One of the last things he said to me was that peace is precious, and we all have to do what we can to preserve it."

When Bob's story trailed off, silence settled on the cellar like a soft blanket. I heard Kevin sniffle. My inner journalist wanted to ask questions, push for more information. But instead Elena broke in, "Way to bum everyone out, Bob."

Bob blinked, as if coming out of a trance, and then actually grinned. "Sorry. That wasn't my intention. Maybe we should get back to the reason you came. It was my constellation book you needed, right?" He popped the lid from a plastic tote and pulled out an oversized hardcover book: *Exploring the Stars: A Seasonal Guide to the New England Sky.* The cover was a photograph of the night sky with lines connecting some of the stars, faint images drawn around them to show what the pictured constellations represented. "Here you go." Bob handed the book to Elena. "Yours to use as long as you need it. This for some sort of school assignment?"

"Uh, yeah," Elena said. She swallowed.

"Kind of a self-directed-study thing," Edgar added.

"Well, I'm glad you selected the stars." Bob winked. "Though as an old astronomer, I may be more than a little biased." His eyes twinkled far more like a jolly Santa than the angry Santa he'd been when we'd first arrived.

We climbed from the cellar and all its unexpected history and said our goodbyes to Bob on the cabin's front porch.

Bob leaned on the porch's railing and cleared his throat. "Don't know if you kids would be interested— probably plenty busy with school and all. But . . . well, there's the Orionid meteor shower coming up in October. It's not usually as spectacular as the more well-known Perseid shower, but it's still pretty special. I'd be happy for you kids to come back, with your parents or whatever, and I'll show it to you with my telescope."

"Mr. H, that would be amazing!" Elena raised her hand for a fist bump.

"Don't forget Saturday," Kevin said, climbing onto his bike. "My speech at the farmers market."

Bob nodded but didn't make any promises.

We turned and waved as we pedaled down Bob Hensworth's driveway, but at White Bend Road, I slammed on my brakes.

"Guys, we have a problem!"

The other GEEKs skidded to a halt beside me. I pointed down.

A half-smoked cigarette lay smoldering on the ground beside Bob's mailbox.

We scanned up and down the road and peered into the surrounding woods. There was no guy in a Yankees cap—or anyone else—in sight. I took out my notebook and jotted a few notes. A reporter never knows when information may prove useful.

"I really don't like this," Kevin said, his voice trembling.

"Me neither," Edgar added. "As Lin-Manuel Miranda once—"

"Not now, Edge," Elena said. "We've got enough

drama without Lin's help. Maybe we should focus on what Bob told us. After all, it *is* pretty cool having an MIT-trained astronomer around."

"Keep your voices down," Kevin said, eyes darting around. "We don't know who might be able to hear us."

"Do you think it's possible Maxine included a clue that could only be decoded in the springtime?" I asked, in a near whisper.

Kevin pursed his lips. "If she did—and if the constellations book doesn't help—it'll be too late to save the factory."

Edgar's lip started to quiver. "And my parents will have to sell Ollie. . . ."

Elena raised her hands. "Let's not lose hope, people. We can still—"

"You're right," Kevin said. "I've got my speech on Saturday. Like Bob said, the important thing is to bring people together. Maybe I can inspire people to start a grassroots movement. If Elmwood achieved so much in the past, surely the town can come together now to find a way to save the factory!"

I wanted to believe Kevin, but I couldn't help picturing the red-stamped FINAL NOTICE paper hidden on Mom's desk. I stepped on the still-smoldering cigarette and ground it into the dirt.

"For starters," Kevin said, "I'll encourage people who were planning to leave not to. The heart of Elmwood was never one rich family—it was all the people who live here. People like Mr. Hensworth and Ms. Kaminski. And if we stay, we can save it together. Maybe we can talk to someone about attracting new businesses here, new investors. In the meantime, we can all volunteer to help each other, organize a fundraiser. . . ."

The spark in Kevin's eye made me feel a little bit better. He clearly cared for Elmwood more than I'd given him credit for. It was the whole reason the election was so important to him. But as he continued to talk through his ideas out loud, I couldn't help but worry that, though he did know how to give a good speech, that was all it was.

I knew the *Elmwood Tribune* had been lucky to stay open as long as it had. That there were small towns just like ours all over the country, slowly emptying out. But who was I to kill Kevin's dreams? The fact that he never gave up trying to make life better for everyone around him, no matter the odds, was what I liked most about him.

Still, my silent doubt hung between us like a curtain until Elena swept it aside: "Hey, GEEKs, I'm starving. How about we test Newton's laws of motion and get our bikes heading toward the Maple Leaf?"

That ended up being the best question any of us had asked all day.

Mrs. Dupree looked up from behind the counter as soon as the bell jangled above the front door. "Four of my favorite people!" she exclaimed when she saw us. "What can I do for you today?"

"After-school hunger emergency, Mrs. D," Elena said.

Edgar clutched his stomach and staggered around the diner. "Save the starving children!"

Mrs. Dupree laughed. "I happen to have fresh apple pie plus some caramel ice cream that needs to be eaten before it gets freezer burned. I also have a bunch of files and boxes I cleared out of storage, and now I need them organized. How about a trade—I start you with pie and ice cream; then you give *me* an hour's worth of help. Deal?"

"Deal!" we all said.

Mrs. Dupree ended up feeding us each *two* slices of warm apple pie plus ice cream, then guided us to her office.

Normally, the tiny office barely had space for Mrs. Dupree's desk and chair and a pair of gray file cabinets. Now we huddled in the doorway, unable to push past the stacks and stacks of boxes crammed into the room.

Mrs. Dupree patted her cloud of white hair. "Sweeties, did I mention how many boxes there were?"

I love the other GEEKs—they're the best friends in the world. But after Mrs. Dupree gave us directions and we spent the next hour sifting, sorting, and organizing boxes, I wished I were working alone. Here are a few facts to help you understand:

FACT #1: Elena detests organization. (Her exact words as she grabbed fistfuls of papers, glanced at them, and then shoved them back into boxes: "The scientific concept of *entropy* explains how the universe moves toward disorder. Why are we trying to battle the universe?")

FACT #2: Kevin loves organization. (His exact words as he tried to straighten the papers Elena had just messed up: "Hold on, Elena! We need to establish a color-coded organizational system to maximize our productivity and efficiency!")

FACT #3: When he's nervous or excited, Edgar often makes up his own Shakespearean quotes. (His exact words—which he repeated every time Kevin and Elena started arguing—"O paperwork, paperwork! Wherefore art thou such a mess?")

Our hour was almost over when I came across a stack of really old bank deposit slips. I was about to move them to our need-to-be-recycled pile when the name of the bank made me pause. More specifically, it was the *star* in the middle—North *Star* Bank.

Kevin and Elena were busy arguing, and Edgar was making another "O paperwork!" proclamation, so I slipped from the office to find Mrs. Dupree.

She was in the kitchen, washing pots and pans.

I held out one of the deposit slips. "Mrs. Dupree, where's this bank?"

"You never heard of North Star, sweetie?" Mrs. Dupree clicked her tongue. "No, I don't suppose you would have. That bank closed even before Maxine Van Houten passed. Haven't you ever wondered what that grand building was across the town square?"

I frowned in confusion. "You mean the Capitol?"

"Is that what you children call the place?" Mrs. Dupree scrubbed at something crusted in the bottom of one of her pans. "I suppose the building does look like a little piece of Washington, DC, shrunk down and brought to Elmwood, doesn't it? But that was North Star for you."

"Don't you mean Premier Mutual?" I offered. "That's what the sign out front says."

"Oh, it *became* Premier Mutual, but before they took over the building, it was North Star Bank for decades. Anyway, now it's neither. They closed our downtown branch and moved it to Grove Park. It's a real shame to have such a beautiful building closed tight." She shook her head. "It had the loveliest painting of the night sky on the domed ceiling. . . ."

I sucked in a breath, then started shooting off questions like newspapers from a printing press: "Is the painting still there? Who created it? Did it show the constellations? Who owns the building? Is there—"

"Whoa, whoa! Slow down," Mrs. Dupree said. "All I can tell you is that Premier Mutual closed the bank and put the building up for sale. Of course, only one person in these parts could afford something so grand. Eventually, Maxine Van Houten bought it, planning to make it a Van Houten Toys store, though she passed before any work began."

"So the painting of the night sky . . . ?"

"Probably still there, hiding under a lot of dust."

"And the owner of the building?"

"I imagine it must be part of the Van Houten estate." Mrs. Dupree squinted at me curiously. "Why so interested in an old, abandoned bank? Chasing another scoop?"

I folded and unfolded the old deposit slip. "A journalist never knows where she'll find her next story." I tried to stay calm, hoping my face didn't give away how important the bank might actually be.

Mrs. Dupree glanced at a clock on the wall above the sink. "Well, you've certainly all earned your pie. Tell your friends I appreciated their help." She waved a dish towel in the direction of the town square and smiled. "Now feel free to go chase some news."

I didn't need a second invitation. "Thanks, Mrs. Dupree!" I dashed to the diner's cramped office.

"O paperwork, paperwork! Wherefore art—"

"Work time's over, GEEKs!" I cried, trying to catch my breath. "Mrs. Dupree says thanks. Now come on. I may know where the Big Bear kisses Jupiter!"

The Elmwood Tribune

Saturday, June 10, 1995

A LION, A DRAGON, AND BEARS . . . OH, MY!

A CLOSER LOOK AT OUR SUMMER SKY

By BOB HENSWORTH

As we near the summer solstice, tonight's sky provides a waxing gibbous moon and much more for any stargazer's enjoyment. Careful inspection can reveal a lion, a dragon, two bears, and even the mythological hero Hercules.

I recommend beginning with a star and constellation you most likely already recognize. First, locate the North Star—Polaris. This bright star is part of Ursa Minor, a constellation you probably call the Little Dipper. It is also known as the Small Bear. Of course, if you have a Small Bear, you must have a Big Bear nearby. The Big Bear is also known as Ursa Major, which includes the well-known Big Dipper.

If you're surprised to find two bears in the night sky, you may be even more surprised to find the constellation that snakes its way between them—Draco the Dragon. . . .

We couldn't risk more trespassing. Especially since the police station sat directly across the street from the old bank. So, when Max didn't answer his phone on Wednesday, we'd had to wait until Thursday afternoon. That's when Max finally responded to a text and agreed to meet us downtown.

Max showed up with a long flashlight tucked under one arm and the huge ring of keys he'd received from Mr. Ridley, the lawyer. He shuffled through key after key, trying to jam one into the lock, mumbling to himself, then moving on to the next.

The other GEEKs and I stood a few yards away at the corner and tried not to look suspicious. Although Edgar is definitely the best actor, I didn't think his whistling-with-his-hands-in-his-pockets approach was the best choice. I kept a sharp eye out for Yankees Man in case he was still tailing us, but only a few townsfolk wandered by.

It was Mrs. Nancy Pringle, the fire chief's wife, who decided to stop and say something.

Mrs. Pringle glared at Max. "Little late to be trying to reopen the bank, don't you think? Who's got money left to keep there?"

Max fumbled the ring of keys. They dropped from his fingers and clanged onto the pavement. "I'm so very sorry," he mumbled.

"Just not sorry enough to do anything about it!" Mrs. Pringle snapped. She stomped off before Max could reply.

Mrs. Pringle was known for her Thanksgiving food drive and her beautiful Christmas lights. I'd never heard her speak to *anyone* that way. It was like the news about the factory had broken her.

Max sighed. He plucked the keys from the ground and restarted his attempt to unlock the bank.

Edgar glanced around and then whispered, "Don't feel bad, Max. If this all works out, people like Mrs. Pringle will find out you've been doing something good all along."

"I hope so, Edgar," Max said, right as he finally found a key that clicked in the lock.

The door scraped as Max pushed it open, swiping a

line through the thick layer of dust on the dark granite floor. He turned on his flashlight. The rest of us flipped on the lights on our phones. Like Maxine's old office at the toy factory, the North Star Bank was a time machine to the 1980s.

A high counter sat like an island in the middle of the lobby, tiny wooden cubbies still holding blank deposit slips. A nearby oak desk had a typewriter on it instead of a computer. There were no ATMs or change-counting machines in sight. However, it was the ceiling that quickly grabbed our attention.

"Oh, sweet Einstein . . . ," Elena murmured.

"Holy constellations . . . ," Kevin said.

Edgar thrust his arms skyward. "'Hung be the heavens with black, yield day to night!'" When Max gave him a funny look, Edgar shrugged and added, "*Henry the Sixth,* act one, scene one."

I just gazed silently upward. A chandelier with a five-pointed-star design hung from the middle of a high, domed ceiling covered completely by a mural of the night sky. We definitely stood "within a shadow of five points."

Elena pulled out the constellations book Bob Hensworth had lent to us. She flipped to a bookmarked page showing Ursa Major — the Big Bear. We all huddled together and studied the book, then shone our lights around the ceiling. Searching. Hoping. Praying.

"There!" Kevin cried. He pointed across the lobby to

a spot near the edge of the ceiling, a little above a high balcony that circled the dome's perimeter.

"Nice work, Kev," Elena said. "Let's go." She took off toward a broad stairway that curved along the lobby's wall. We followed, the slap of our sneakers echoing through the bank.

Elena led us around the balcony to the spot where Kevin had seen the Big Bear. We all focused our lights on the large constellation. This time, Edgar was the first to point and say, "Is that it?"

There—tucked among the Big Bear's stars, above a narrow ledge at the juncture of the domed ceiling and wall—was Jupiter. Edgar, who was taller than all of us, tried to reach the ledge, but even he wasn't tall enough.

Kevin stepped forward. "I can get on your shoulders."

He was shaking slightly, but clearly determined to overcome his fear of heights. I couldn't help but be proud of him then.

"Wait . . . we need to be very careful here," said Max, eyeing the fall from the balcony railing. "Kevin, you look a bit, well, shaky. I don't want you to lose your balance. And besides, Gina is probably lighter. Easier for Edgar to lift."

Kevin frowned, but there was no arguing with facts. It made more sense for me to do it.

"I got it, Kev," I said gently. "You'll get the next one."

Edgar knelt down, and I climbed on. Kevin and

Elena helped balance me as Edgar stood back up. Edgar positioned himself along the wall, and I stretched as high as possible. My fingers brushed along the ledge. Dust rained onto my face, making me sneeze. My body jerked.

Edgar wobbled slightly but regained his balance. "Careful," he said.

I reached up again, turning my face to avoid the dust. My fingers poked and patted.

"Anything?" Kevin asked.

"No," I said, "not yet." My blind search continued. The Big Bear kissing Jupiter . . . This had to be it. . . . Then my fingertips brushed something soft. "Hold on, I think . . . there's something here!"

I pulled down a dusty, zippered deposit bag. Gold letters stamped into the cracked, brown leather read: VAN HOUTEN TOY & GAME CO.

31

"Open it, open it!" Elena cried as Edgar lowered me to the floor.

My fingers shook as I unzipped the pouch. I don't think any of us dared breathe. I reached inside and pulled out a single sheet of paper, which contained now-familiar typewriter lettering:

A town has a heartbeat,

A soul, and a voice.

After flames passed through Elmwood,

This town made a choice—

To restore its own speech,

To let it be free.

Find the Girl with the Red Scarf—

'86 holds the key.

At the bottom of the page was an extra message: *Only two clues left to find!*

After some excited babbling, we descended from the balcony and exited the bank, discussing the clue as we went.

"What the heck does it mean by 'the Girl with the Red Scarf'?" Elena asked.

Kevin pointed to the clue's last line. "Eighty-six is written like a year. So maybe that's 1986. But how would we find a red-scarfed girl from nearly four decades ago?"

"I'm not sure," Edgar said, "but the 'flames passed through Elmwood' part could be about the fire that damaged the theater in the 1980s."

"I'm just glad I have you kids to help." Max paused to relock the doors. "Without you, I never would have—"

"*There* you are!" a voice growled.

We all jumped, but Elena went the highest. Her dad— Police Chief Luis Hernández—was stomping across the street from the police station, his lips a thin, rigid line.

"Hiya, Papá," Elena said, her voice tight. "I—"

"Mrs. Pringle said I might find you here. You were grounded! Remember that, hija? Grounded!"

"Papá, I—"

"I specifically told you—straight home after school. Every day. Straight. Home. Then today—*poof!* I discover you've been lying to your abuela and sneaking around behind our backs while your mother and I have been working long hours."

"Papá, if you'd just let me—"

"And *you!*" Elena's dad glared at Max. "What do you think you're doing hanging out with a bunch of kids? Are you the one who put them up to their stunt at the theater?"

Max spluttered. "Me? No. I—well—I only—"

"This is my fault, Papá," Elena said. "I'm writing a paper about the old bank building for social studies. I found out Max had keys to the place and talked him into letting us take a look inside."

"Yes, that's right, Officer," Max said, picking up Elena's story. He focused on the keys in his hands, not meeting Chief Hernández's angry gaze. "It was my first time in the building—I've been quite busy since I got to town—but I wanted to be a good neighbor during my time in Elmwood."

Chief Hernández folded his arms across his thick chest. "Then I think you've been more than neighborly enough for one day. How about moving along now?"

"Yes, Officer. Absolutely." Max bobbed his head

217

like a nervous chicken. "I'm sure the kids will be fine on their own from here. Glad I could help them out, but sorry for the confusion. I certainly never meant to—"

"Move along." Chief Hernández's left eyelid twitched. *"Now."*

Max scampered down the stairs and shot across to Van Houten Park.

Elena's dad refocused on her. "Hija, I'll be taking you home, which is a place you'll be staying every non-school minute of every day for the foreseeable future." Then he turned to the rest us. "I expect more from the rest of you, too."

Kevin hung his head. "We're sorry, sir."

"You never told us you were grounded!" I whispered to Elena.

"Sorry," Elena whispered back. "Was I supposed to let you solve the puzzle without me?"

"You could've been honest with us," I said.

I don't know what Elena would have said next, because right then, her dad opened the front passenger's door of his cruiser and motioned Elena inside. I gave her a glum wave.

"It looks like we're down one GEEK now," I said, as the Hernándezes drove off. "The three of us can meet after school tomorrow to figure out the new clue."

Kevin studied his fingernails. "Tomorrow's the last

day before my big speech, so I really need the time to prepare."

Edgar puckered his lips. I figured he was about to tell Kevin how crazy it was to be worrying about a speech when we had a hidden fortune to hunt down. Instead, Edgar said, "With all our hunting down of clues, I need to catch up on some schoolwork, plus I have a drama club meeting after school tomorrow." He tugged on one of his loopy curls. "Sorry . . ."

"Seriously, you two? We're searching for the next-to-last clue, and you suddenly want to take a break?"

"I know the treasure is important," Kevin said. "But my speech has a deadline that's less than forty-eight hours away, and our treasure hunt doesn't."

I couldn't believe I had to have this conversation! "What about Yankees Man? We keep seeing cigarette butts all over town, and Max says he's getting harassing calls. *Someone* else is looking for this treasure, and we can't let them beat us to it!"

"I know someone else is searching for the treasure," said Kevin, scuffing the stairs with his shoe, "but think about it—*we* have all the clues, not him. He has no way to get to the next clue without us. Skipping one day won't matter. Besides, you can still be thinking about the clue. Just don't go chasing after anything on your own. We'll pick it up as a team after my speech on Saturday. No big deal."

"Fine," I mumbled.

We were getting so close, it was hard to let things go, even for a single day. But I vowed I'd be patient.

Then Friday came, and I found out how little time was actually left.

The Elmwood Tribune

Wednesday, February 11, 1987

ICONIC DOWNTOWN LANDMARK SAVED BY THE TOYS

By RAMONA LEE

When the Blaze of '85 swept through downtown Elmwood, the luck of a shifting breeze saved the vacated North Star Bank building. Two years later, the building has been saved once again. However, instead of a breeze from Mother Nature doing the saving, this time it's Elmwood's own beloved whirlwind—Maxine Van Houten.

Local real estate records reveal that Van Houten, the CEO of Van Houten Toy & Game Company, recently purchased the historic North Star Bank building in downtown Elmwood, which has been vacant since shortly after North Star's merger with Premier Mutual Bank in 1980. When Van Houten was asked about her plans for the building, she said, "Van Houten Toys will finally have its own store, and I can think of no finer site for our flagship location than the beautiful building that was long the home of North Star Bank. The store will not only serve as a showcase for our fine toys, but will be an exciting, interactive destination that will continue to draw people into our community." . . .

32

After school on Friday, Elena was punished with in-home lockdown, Kevin went to work on his speech, and Edgar had drama club. I went home and found chaos.

My mom sat cross-legged on the floor of the newsroom, surrounded by boxes, large black trash bags, and piles of newspapers and miscellaneous junk. "Bean," she said, "boy, am I glad to see you!" She brushed a stray strand of hair from her face, accidentally leaving a smear of newsprint across her cheek.

"What are you doing, Mom?"

"Sorting." Mom held up a chipped coffee mug that had *The Elmwood Tribune* written on the side in fancy script. "Frankie has room for *us* in her apartment. Not for all our stuff."

"Since when are we moving for sure?" I asked, biting my lower lip. I didn't need another reminder that I could be forced out of Elmwood and hauled off to Massachusetts.

Mom's face grew serious. "There are some things I need to tell you about. Some updates." Mom set down the chipped coffee mug. "I've officially been offered the job in Boston."

I blinked. "But you're not taking it. Not yet. Right?"

"I have to give Beantown Lifestyle Living my answer by Wednesday."

My mind ticked through the calendar. "That's only five days away!"

"Yes."

"So tell them you need more time."

"That's the problem, Gina Bean." Mom pulled out the paper I'd seen on her desk one week earlier. "We don't really have more time."

The FINAL NOTICE at the top of the page turned to a red blur as tears stung my eyes. "What—what is it?" I whispered, sinking onto the floor beside my mom.

"You know I bought the newspaper with the money from your father's life insurance policy, and that kept us going quite a while. But the newspaper has struggled. I had to get a loan from the bank." Mom traced a finger absently over the FINAL NOTICE. "Payment is overdue."

This couldn't be happening. Not with the GEEKs so

close to finding the lost fortune! I drew a shaky breath. "Can't you ask the bank for an extension?"

Mom shook her head. "They've already given me an extension." She smoothed the bank notice over her lap. "Twice. If I haven't made a payment on the loan by October first, the bank will take possession of the *Elmwood Tribune*."

"But that's next Friday!"

Mom nodded. "Which is why on Wednesday I plan to accept the job in Boston."

I sat, stunned, barely able to breathe. I'd thought the GEEKs' search for the Van Houten fortune was mostly a race against Yankees Man. Now it was a race against job offers and bank loans, and Mom was five days away from sealing our fates and dragging me away from Elmwood forever.

Mom set the bank notice aside and rubbed my back. "I know this is very sudden, Bean, but things will work out. You'll see." She patted a stack of yellowed newspapers. "In the meantime, can I get you to sort through these old papers to see if there are any worth keeping?"

They're all worth keeping! I wanted to scream, but I no longer had the energy to argue. I rubbed at my eyes. "Sure, Mom." I started searching for any interesting headlines, hunting for excuses to keep as many papers as possible. I was picking up a brittle, yellowed copy of the *Elmwood Tribune* from 1988 when the newspaper's slogan—printed right below the newspaper's name— caught my eye.

It read: *The Voice of Elmwood.*

I fumbled for my phone, which included a photo of the clue from the bank. Parts of the clue leapt at me: *A town has a heartbeat, a soul, and a voice . . . To restore its own speech, to let it be free.*

The town's voice . . . free speech . . . I read the motto again. Every journalist knows that freedom of speech and freedom of the press are at the heart and soul of the First Amendment to the United States Constitution. In Elmwood, the *Elmwood Tribune* embodied that heart and soul—it was the town's voice!

My heart pounded. "Mom?"

"Yes, Bean?"

"I know a fire happened in Elmwood a long time ago, but when was it? And what happened, exactly?" I shuffled a couple of newspapers around, trying to look like I was still working instead of just holding my breath, waiting for her reply.

"Ah, you're referring to the Blaze of Eighty-Five." Mom tossed a few nubby pencils into one of the garbage bags. "The fire started in Emily's Antiques because of faulty wiring in an old lamp. Unfortunately, it was a windy day. The fire leapt from building to building, decimating almost the entire downtown area—the old library, the theater, even the original *Elmwood Tribune* office. Luckily, a sudden shift in the wind spared the east side of the town square—town hall and the old bank building."

"What did the town do after the fire?" I asked.

"You realize I was only in elementary school at the time, right?"

I moved another couple of newspapers into my "keep" pile. "You were born to be a journalist, Mom. Like me. I'm betting you paid attention."

Mom laughed. "You're right, Bean. I suppose I did pay a bit more attention to things around town than most other kids." She gazed off across the room. "Some businesses downtown had struggled even before the fire. The Maple Grove Mall had opened out by the highway, and more and more people did their shopping there. Then the fire hit, and a lot of the businesses that burned didn't have adequate insurance and couldn't afford to rebuild. In fact, the *Elmwood Tribune* got folded into the *Grove Park Herald* for nearly two years."

After flames passed through Elmwood . . .

"A lot of people didn't think it was even worth rebuilding," Mom continued. "Then Maxine Van Houten got involved. She said it was vital to preserve the town's history. To 'never forget' what made us Elmwood. She launched a massive fundraising effort she called

Elevate Elmwood, and she convinced the townspeople to follow her lead."

This town made a choice . . .

"Maxine spent plenty of her own money to help, but she also wanted people to feel ownership of the new spaces. She wanted them actively involved. The town put together productions in the park to raise money for the theater. There was a festival at Bamboozle-land, with proceeds going to the worst-hit businesses. My mom and I even baked cookies and sold them outside the Maple Grove Mall to help buy new books for the town library." Mom swiped a thumb beneath one of her eyes. "Not only did the whole town help rebuild downtown, but we managed to split the *Elmwood Tribune* back off from the *Grove Park Herald* so we could have our own town newspaper again."

To restore its own speech, to let it be free.

Mom ran a finger slowly around the rim of the chipped coffee mug, which still sat beside her on the floor. "I know you don't want to move. I get it. When your dad and I got married after college and he got stationed in Cape Cod, I missed Elmwood terribly. Then the helicopter accident . . . the life insurance . . ." Mom sniffled. "Being able to move back here and keep the newspaper running and raise you in the same town where I grew up saved me from a dark place, Bean. It's hard to think about leaving again. This town is a special place . . . or it was."

"It's *still* a special place!" I argued. "So why give up? Why not launch a fundraiser like Maxine Van Houten did?"

Mom rubbed the back of her neck. "In the eighties, the Bamboozler was at the height of its popularity. We had the factory and the good jobs that came with it. Now the factory's going to close, plus we don't have Maxine Van Houten *or* her fortune to get things rolling." Mom pointed to the bank notice. "And, of course, there's *that* little problem."

I wanted to give my mom the facts. Let her know we could have Maxine's fortune to help us. All we had to do was find it.

But I held the secret close. I had five days before Mom was going to accept the job in Boston—five days to find and solve the final clues. My mind spun around the Girl with the Red Scarf. She must have appeared in the *Elmwood Tribune* in 1986, after the newspaper reopened. Did my pile of old papers date back that far?

I started digging.

1988 . . . 1987 . . .

And then I found it. A series of newspapers from

December 1986. The oldest of them—the Sunday, December 7, edition—proudly declared: HOMETOWN PAPER COMES HOME!

I began my hunt for the Girl with the Red Scarf.

An hour later, I admitted defeat.

No photo, headline, article, or advertisement ever mentioned or showed a girl with a red scarf. I had copies of all the original 1986 newspapers after "the Voice of Elmwood" had been restored, and they were just another dead end.

My friends distracted. Mom's job offer. The overdue bank loan. Now this. Everything pressed in on me, each weight added to the one before.

What was I doing wrong? Where was the next clue? And why was I the only one searching?

Mom glanced over. "You must really be interested in those old papers." She batted me playfully on the arm. "Feeling nostalgic?"

I dropped the newspaper I was holding and met my mom's eyes. Then I burst into tears.

"Oh, Gina Bean . . ." Mom pulled me to her chest and rocked gently back and forth. Her fingers ran slowly through the hair that had fallen from my bun. Her fleece sweatshirt pressed against my cheek. "I know it's hard right now," she whispered. "But whatever happens, it will be all right. *We'll* be all right. . . ."

I didn't say anything, just continued to let my mom rock me like a baby in her arms. *Maybe Mom's right,* I told myself, my tearful waterfall slowing to a trickle. *There are worse places to live than Boston. And there's still a chance we won't have to move. Maybe Kevin's speech really could motivate the town, just like Maxine did back in the eighties. . . .*

Even after my tears stopped completely, Mom stayed there on the floor of the newsroom, holding me, rocking me, whispering promises. Then finally she said, "Hey, Bean, how about an early dinner of ice cream sundaes and a few episodes of *Gilmore Girls*?"

I sniffled. With my face still pressed against Mom's shoulder, my reply was muffled: "We can't watch *Gilmore Girls*. I'm grounded from TV, remember?"

Mom stroked my hair. "I think tonight warrants an exception. What do you say?"

What I said was yes.

By the time I crawled into bed hours later, my stomach was full to bursting with vanilla ice cream, caramel sauce, and rainbow sprinkles, but even *Gilmore Girls* hadn't been able to clear my mind of unsolvable clues and hidden treasures. When I finally drifted into sleep, my dreams were haunted by moving trucks stamped on the sides with BOSTON — FINAL NOTICE.

But as the horizon pinkened from the rising sun, it

wasn't my dreams that snapped me awake. It was the clue.

I knew where to find the Girl with the Red Scarf!

It was only six a.m. on a Saturday, but I grabbed my phone. There was one other GEEK who'd already be awake.

33

I explained to Edgar what I'd figured out. Then, to hustle him along, I went to help him with his farm chores.

Edgar claims that when you live on a dairy farm, you get used to the smell. Believe me—that's nothing to brag about. I was glad our work was done at nine a.m.

I showed Edgar the Grove Park Library's hours on my phone. "The library's just now opening. It won't take long to get there on our bikes. Then we'll have about two hours before we need to pedal back to Elmwood for Kevin's speech."

Edgar peered out of the barn, making sure we were alone, even though he knew his parents had already left to set up their booth at the farmers market. "My mom and dad will kill me if they find out. You know I'm only allowed to ride around town."

"They'll still be at the farmers market when we get back. They'll never know."

"Kevin and Elena will be mad if we go without them."

"No way can we let Elena sneak out again," I said. "And you heard Kevin yesterday. He'll just want to focus on preparing his speech."

"We could wait until he's done."

"No!" I hadn't meant to snap, but Mom's Boston-job countdown clock kept tick-ticking in my head, even though I hadn't worked up the nerve to tell Edgar about it. I had to find the treasure before Wednesday! I grabbed my backpack off a nearby hay bale and slung it over my shoulders. "I'm going. Your only choice is whether you're making me go alone."

Edgar sighed. "You know, Gina, sometimes you're even pushier than Elena." But he smiled when he said it. And he went to fetch his bike.

Grove Park had fared better than Elmwood over the years, and it showed. As we rode over the Elmgrove Bridge, which joined our towns over the White Bend River, we had to squint against the sun reflecting off Grove Park's shiny buildings. One of the executives the Van Houten family had fired after Maxine died had gone on to found some kind of tech company in Grove Park. Apparently, it had done pretty well.

The library there was much bigger than ours, and it had been designed by some fancy architect. We arrived—sweaty and out of breath—around nine-fifteen. We locked our bikes to the rack and hurried for the door.

What I'd realized that morning—what had yanked me from my sleep—was the fact that Maxine's treasure hunt must have taken months and months to create. When she'd written the clue about the Girl with the Red Scarf, she knew the *Elmwood Tribune* was being restored, but that didn't mean it had actually happened yet. What if she'd placed the clue right *before* the newspaper reopened? What if she'd placed it in the only local paper left after the Blaze of '85? What if the Girl with the Red Scarf was hiding in the *Grove Park Herald*?

As soon as I walked through the door, I went up to a teenage girl who was reshelving a cart full of books. "Excuse me," I said. "Do you have old copies of the *Grove Park Herald*?"

The girl popped a bubble of pink gum that matched the pink streak of dye in her hair. "There," she said, her voice flat and bored. She waved a hand vaguely toward the other end of the library, then picked a book from her cart, checked the label on its spine, and slid it onto the shelf.

"Do the papers date back to 1986?"

The girl clicked her tongue and rolled her eyes. "You want the *archives*?"

"Yes, that's it!" I said. "The archives—the archives from 1986."

"What month?"

I forced a smile. "Um . . . all of them?"

"It's for a school project," Edgar added. "Local history stuff."

The girl sighed heavily. "Wait here."

By the time she reappeared ten minutes later, Edgar and I were about to go crazy from waiting. She pushed a rattly cart piled high with newspapers.

"Thank you," I said. "Thanks so much."

"No prob," the girl replied. She snapped her gum. "Just keep them in order." She trudged back to her cart of books.

Edgar and I were the only people visiting the library that early on a Saturday, so we wheeled our cart over to a blue couch in the children's section.

"I asked for the whole year," I said, "but the *Tribune* reopened in December, so let's start with November."

We each grabbed a paper from November 1986. The masthead said:

The Grove Park Herald

**Serving the Fair Valley communities
of Grove Park, Briar Lake & Elmwood**

I was so used to our tiny Elmwood newspaper, I hadn't thought about how much thicker a newspaper would be that served three towns, especially since both Grove Park and Briar Lake are larger than Elmwood. Our search was slow, the only sounds the crinkle and rustle of newspaper pages and an occasional grunt or sigh from me or Edgar.

We looked for headlines about a girl in a red scarf. We studied every photograph and caption. We skimmed articles. We browsed the classified ads. The stack of papers that didn't have the clue slowly grew. The morning ticked by: 10:40 . . . 10:50 . . . eleven o'clock.

We had to find the clue, and we had to find it fast! Kevin's speech was at eleven-thirty, which was fast approaching. He'd kill us if we missed it.

11:05 . . .

I moved backward into the October editions.

11:10 . . .

Edgar moved forward into the December editions.

11:15 . . . "Gina, look!" Edgar leapt up. He shook a newspaper over his head. "The Girl with the Red Scarf!"

"Shhh!" I yanked Edgar back down onto the couch. "Show me."

It was right there in the classifieds of the Friday, December 5, 1986, edition of the *Grove Park Herald*. I should have known the clue would be in the last edition of the paper before the *Tribune* reopened! The personal ad stated:

To the Girl with the Red Scarf: Unlock the fun and find the treasure. I wish you well. –M.

" 'Unlock the fun and find the treasure'—that's the slogan for the Bamboozler," I said.

Edgar groaned. "You made me ride a bike to Grove Park just to find the Bamboozler slogan?"

I had to admit, I was hoping for something a little more detailed. "But at least I was right—the clue was here."

"Yeah, but . . ." Edgar looked at his phone. "We have to go! Kevin's speech is in ten minutes!"

"You're right," I said. "He'll kill us if we're late."

"He'll kill us if we aren't early!"

Edgar snapped a photo of the clue, and we hurriedly restacked the papers onto the cart before dashing out the door.

As I fumbled with the lock on our bikes, a horn honked. A stranger with a graying beard and a floppy, tan newsboy cap sat in a silver sedan. He rolled his window down and waved us over. "Excuse me? Kids?" he called in a raspy voice. "Can you help me a minute?"

"We don't really have a minute," I whispered to Edgar.

Edgar—who is sometimes too nice for his own good—said, "You get our bikes. I'll see what he wants."

"Well, just don't get in his car or anything stupid like that," I said.

Edgar gave me a *Thank you very much, Gina Sparks, but I am not six years old* look before heading toward the car.

As I unhooked our bikes, I heard the man explaining to Edgar. "I'm late for an important doctor's appointment," he said, "but I got all turned around, and of course my phone is dead. Could I possibly borrow your phone to call the office? I know I'm close. . . ."

We *really* needed to go! I hurried both our bikes over as Edgar told the man, "Sure."

As Edgar began to hand over his phone, the man reached out for it a bit too quickly. His arm brushed against his face, knocking part of his beard loose.

Wait. What? I blinked. "Edgar . . ."

That's when I noticed the stink of cigarettes in the air.

And the Yankees cap sitting on the passenger seat.

34

"Edgar! No!" I let go of our bikes and lunged for Edgar's arm.

He reflexively pulled his phone back.

The man's hand shot from the open car window. "Give me that!"

His fingers brushed against Edgar's phone, but Edgar kept his grip.

"Ride!" I said, jerking my bike from the sidewalk. "It's *him*!"

I could see the question clouding Edgar's eyes, even as he pocketed his phone and grabbed his bike.

"Not so fast!" the man growled. He began to open his door. His fake beard hung half on and half off, like he was a zombie with a melting face.

"The guy!" I added, straddling my seat. "Yankees Man!"

Understanding flashed across Edgar's face. We barreled down the sidewalk, pedals pumping.

A car door slammed. Tires squealed.

I didn't dare look back.

Edgar and I shot from the library's parking lot and veered onto a side street. A red pickup truck blared its horn and screeched to a halt, its chrome bumper missing me by inches. I didn't stop.

My bike chain creaked. My legs spun. Edgar's breath huffed in and out as he struggled to keep pace.

A car engine roared behind us.

"To the right!" I cut across someone's flower bed, raced along the side of the house, and skidded into an alley. Edgar was right on my tail. We flew down the alley, gravel crunching under our bike tires. We were a dozen yards from the alley's exit when the silver sedan stopped in front of us.

"Brake!" Edgar screamed.

I didn't need the advice. I punched down on my brakes. My bike skittered and skidded, lurching sideways. I swayed a split second, then regained control.

The silver car screeched into a tight turn and sped toward us down the narrow alley.

This time, it was Edgar who took the lead. "I may not live to see tomorrow," he hollered, "but I will gladly join the fight!" Then he took off . . . *heading straight at the car!*

What in the Hamilton?

I'm not sure what I was thinking, but I followed him.

In case you ever consider playing a bike-versus-car game of chicken, please note—it's absolutely terrifying.

Just before Edgar became a hood ornament, he swerved left. His handlebars nearly clipped the car's side-view mirror. Then he was through.

I wasn't far behind. Dust from Edgar's churning tires kicked up into my face. I blinked my eyes clear. My handlebars scraped the car's passenger-side door. I wobbled. Then I was through too.

Yankees Man shrieked a bunch of words that don't belong in a family newspaper. We didn't stick around to see how long it would take him to back out of the narrow alley.

Edgar led us across yards, down more alleys, and through a variety of twisting side streets until we ended up on a path through some woods. We kept going, heading in the general direction of Elmwood.

But then . . . *Pop!*

Edgar's chugging, churning legs slowed, and he coasted to a stop. The redness that always flushed his cheeks had taken over his entire face. Sweat poured from under his bike helmet. His curly hair lay plastered to his forehead.

Edgar pointed toward the back of his bike. "Got a flat," he wheezed. A steady hiss sounded from his rear tire. "But I think we lost Yankees Man."

"Yeah," I said. My legs burned, and I struggled for my own breath. "Thanks to you." Then I slugged Edgar in the arm. "But if you *ever* go all *Hamilton* brave like that again, I'll kill you myself if the car doesn't do it first!"

Edgar grinned and waggled his eyebrows. He puffed his chest out like some brave knight. "To quote Lin-Manue—"

"Let's find a way out of here. Maybe we can make it for the end of Kevin's speech."

Edgar pulled out his phone. He moaned, his grin fading. *"No service."*

It was afternoon by the time Edgar and I pushed our bikes into Elmwood, exhausted, sweaty, and starving. Edgar's rear tire half rolled, half scraped along the ground. My bike basket—which had snagged on a branch in the woods—flapped like a wounded bird from one side of my handlebars.

As we hobbled through downtown, the town square sat empty and quiet, the farmers market long since packed away. Other than our own shuffling, scraping progress, the only sounds were a handful of birds and a faint rustling of leaves in the afternoon breeze. Then I heard the thwack.

I stopped and held up a hand. "Did you hear that?"

Edgar cocked his head to one side. I could tell he heard it too—a slow but steady *thwack-thwack* coming from the park. It took a moment before we spotted Kevin huddled in the shadow of Maxine Van Houten, beating a stick over and over against her statue's base.

Despite our tiredness, we rushed toward him. "Kevin," I cried, "we're so sorry!"

Kevin pulled his knees tighter to his chest without raising his head. He kept pounding the stick against the statue, a handful of papers clutched in his other hand.

"Kevin," Edgar said, "you won't believe—"

"You're right," Kevin snapped. "I won't." His head came up. His eyes were red and puffy. "I had a speech, an *important* speech"—he shook the papers he was holding—"and you didn't bother to show up."

"Kevin, we—"

"In fact, hardly *anybody* bothered showing up!"

Oh no . . . "Kev—"

"My mom and dad. And four other people who I think came just to make fun of me."

"Who would do that?" I cried.

"It doesn't matter," he said bitterly. "The point is, there were six people there. That was it—six people.

Six. And family doesn't count." Kevin's lips quivered. "I stood in the gazebo, talking to air for ten minutes, figuring you guys were just running late. Obviously, I should have realized you actually just didn't care about what I had to say."

"Would you let me—"

"Bob Hensworth showed up toward the end. But still . . . my parents and maybe Bob Hensworth were the only ones who came to hear what I had to say. That doesn't exactly add up to a grassroots movement to save Elmwood."

"But Edgar and I—"

"Oh, don't worry, Gina! I know what you and Edgar did—you went for a bike ride." Kevin practically spit the words *bike ride*. He lurched to his feet. "And you know who told me? Sophina. *Sophina* told me! She said she'd seen the two of you pedaling out of town this morning." Kevin's whole body was shaking now. "So what was the emergency, Gina? Did your new best friend Max need you to run an errand for him?"

"If you would just listen!" I cried just as Kevin snapped his stick across his knee before flinging it and his speech papers to the ground.

"Maybe this town isn't even worth saving. It doesn't even want to save itself. It's over!"

I thought of all we'd learned about our town those

last few days, like how it had pulled together to rebuild from the fire. I thought of the incredible people we'd met, like Ms. Kaminski and Bob Hensworth. How could Kevin say Elmwood wasn't worth saving?

Edgar stepped forward. "Come on, Kevin. It's not over."

"Yeah," I said, "we didn't mean to miss your speech, Kevin. But I've been trying to tell you—Yankees Man chased us! In a car! We had to ride through the woods, and Edgar got a flat tire, and we ended up walking home." I gestured toward our messed-up bikes. "But . . . we found the last clue."

Edgar pulled the photo of the clue up on his phone. "It says, 'To the Girl with the Red Scarf: Unlock the fun and find the treasure. I wish you well. M.'"

I thought the news of our discovery would shake Kevin from his anger. It didn't.

"Great," Kevin said sarcastically. "The Bamboozler slogan. *That's* super helpful." He rolled his eyes. "Did Maxine lead us on this wild goose chase as some kind of Bamboozler advertisement? That is, if it really *was* Maxine who created the treasure hunt in the first place and *if* Max is who he says he is." Kevin started stomping toward home.

"Kevin," I called, "wait up!" We followed after him. Edgar's flat tire scraped along, while my basket swung by one strap and slapped against my bike. "We have proof that Max is who he says he is! We can still find the treasure!"

"I knew the mathematical probability of a hidden treasure was low." Kevin kept walking. I had to run to keep up. "But I wanted to believe. I *forced* myself to believe. I even wanted to believe in Max. Like he was some magical Elmwood fairy godfather or something."

"But we're so close," I said, my voice begging.

Kevin stuffed his hands in his pockets. "My dad says after Christmas we may move closer to his family. I'll probably be at a new school in January. So it doesn't matter that I'm going to lose the election. Maybe I'll make some actual friends in Chicago."

Kevin's words stung like a smack to the face.

"We *are* your friends," Edgar said.

Kevin glared. "I had a speech and you blew it off. I don't owe you *anything*." He spun around and stormed off.

My eyes burned. We'd found a clue, but it had cost us a GEEK. It was a terrible price to pay.

35

I took Sauce with me to the Lookout on Sunday morning. I needed time alone to think, but I also needed Sauce's floppy ears and wagging tail to keep me company. Once we'd settled onto the Lookout's wooden deck, I pulled out my notebook, where I'd copied down the latest clue.

Unlock the fun and find the treasure. I wish you well.

What could the Bamboozler's slogan have to do with an actual treasure? Did Maxine hide a clue inside a specific Bamboozler? If so, how in the world would we ever find it? It wasn't like we could check inside every Bamboozler ever produced.

I scratched Sauce between his ears, and he started snoring. I let my mind wander. I tried imagining where there might be a Bamboozler Maxine could have hidden something inside. I pulled the pencil from my hair bun and started listing all the places in Elmwood where I had seen Bamboozlers.

At first I thought of Van Houten Park—the bronze statue of Maxine with a Bamboozler tucked under one arm. But I'd climbed all over that statue over the years as I'd surveyed the town, searching for scoops. I knew it was a dead end. If there were any secret compartments or hidden hollows, I would have found them long ago.

We hadn't seen any Bamboozlers in the theater or in the old bank building. My mind drifted some more. Mrs. Dupree had Bamboozlers on display at the Maple Leaf. . . .

Unlock the fun and find the treasure. I wish you well. I wish you well. . . .

"That's it!" I leapt to my feet.

Sauce snapped awake and started running miniature laps around the Lookout's deck.

I left the preserve and called Edgar as soon as my cell signal returned, explaining what I'd figured out. Next, I tried Kevin. My heart thumped as the phone rang. It was still early enough that I didn't think he would be at church yet, but . . . there was no answer. I remembered what he'd said yesterday. *Maybe this town isn't even worth saving. . . . Maybe I'll make some actual friends in Chicago.* I chewed my lip. I knew we'd hurt Kevin, and bad. Had he really given up on the treasure? On us?

Finally, I called Elena and told her, too, explaining why we really needed her help. "I know it's a big risk if your dad catches you, but . . ."

"Seriously, Gee? Of course I'm gonna help. We're about to find the final clue! Let's meet up at six o'clock. That's when my abuela watches the news on TV, and my parents are headed out of town on some errand later today. I'm in this like pickles in a toaster!"

Pickles in a toaster totally made no sense, but I let it slide. I was more worried about Elena getting busted. If she got caught, I was afraid the next step for her—and maybe for *all* of us—would be actual jail.

"You kids back again?" Cy asked as Elena, Edgar, and I coasted to stops by the guardhouse at Van Houten Toys.

Elena smiled. "All this factory-closing stress has made my mom super forgetful. Just this morning, she looked at me and called me . . . um . . . Bob!"

Cy laughed. "All right . . . *Bob.*" He winked at Elena. "What did your mom forget this time?"

Elena shook her head. "Her phone. Can you believe it?"

"Guess I'll let you in." The large gate rattled open. "But be quick. It's getting late."

"Don't worry, Cy," Elena said. "We'll be like lightning."

Cy waved as we took off through the gate.

As she had on our last trip, Elena scanned her mom's ID and the lock clicked open. It was time to test my hunch.

Obviously, there was an almost never-ending supply of Bamboozlers at Van Houten Toys, but I was only interested in one of them. And it wasn't even a real Bamboozler. We hurried to the middle of the dark foyer.

"It has to be here." I stepped into the broken, dried-up fountain. My feet kicked a couple of coins that had been tossed there long ago. The coins skittered and clinked across the fountain's dusty, tiled bottom. I smiled. It was those old pennies and nickels that had helped me figure out the clue in the first place.

In addition to the Bamboozler's slogan, Maxine's clue had said, *I wish you well.* Once my brain locked onto that sentence, it was obvious what she'd meant: *I wish you well . . .* a *wishing well.* When the fountain had been filled with water, visitors to Van Houten Toys would toss in coins and make wishes, like it was a wishing well. Elena, Edgar, and I crossed the fountain, stepped onto the low central pedestal, and started examining the supersized metal sculpture of a Bamboozler.

Since I was the shortest, I checked the Bamboozler's base. I ran my hands across the cool metal of the sphere, checking for any seams that might reveal a hidden door. I used the light on my phone, studying the metal rods, tugging at them, hoping one would pull free. Edgar did the same around the middle of the sculpture. Elena scampered to the top of the ten-foot sphere like a toddler on a playground.

"Careful!" I warned her.

"Pfff!" Elena hung from the top by one hand and waved off my concerns with the other. "Always."

I had plenty of facts to disprove Elena's "always" claim, but I didn't have time to argue.

We continued our hunt, tugging, tapping, and checking every inch of the sculpture. This *had* to be the right Bamboozler! Somewhere it must have a—

"I found something!" Elena cried. She was pulling on the top of the sculpture. "One of the Bamboozler rods is missing up here, and there's some little nubby thing in its place."

Shhhing! The foyer hummed with the sound of metal sliding against metal.

Elena stood up, a silver cylinder clutched in one fist. "I am Lady Elena, Warrior Scientist!" She thrust the cylinder toward the ceiling in triumph, then started swinging it like a sword. That's when she lost her balance. "Ahhh!" Elena tottered sideways. Her arms windmilled. The cylinder flew from her hand and arced into the air.

"I've got you!" Edgar and I both called. We dove to catch Elena.

She fell.

"Oof!" Elena hammered into us like a game of whack-a-mole at the county fair.

CLANG! The sound of the cylinder rang through the foyer.

"Hey!" an angry voice shouted. "You ain't supposed to play on that!" Cy came chugging toward us, his shoes clippity-clipping on the tile floor.

Elena, Edgar, and I scrabbled to our feet. The silver cylinder glinted in the bottom of the fountain, ten feet to my left.

"You kids know better," Cy said, a scowl on his usually cheerful face. "I'm disappointed."

We hung our heads, though I also took a step sideways, blocking Cy's view of the cylinder.

"You need to go home," Cy said. "No more monkey business." He pointed at Elena. "Come Monday, I'm afraid I'm gonna have to tell your mother about this."

"No! Please!" Elena didn't need to be an actor to pull tears into her eyes.

Cy crossed his arms. "I know the factory's hard up, but for however long it's open, I gotta keep my job."

"I'm super sorry," Elena said. "We didn't mean any trouble. We were just playing around."

Cy rubbed his chin.

While he was focused on Elena, I took a few more steps sideways, then bent over, fake-tying my shoe. I snatched up the cylinder and shoved it into the waistband of my jeans. It pressed cold and hard against my side. I tugged my sweatshirt over the top of it and stood back up.

Edgar hid his hand by his side and gave me a thumbs-up.

Cy sighed. "I mean, I get it—the factory's closin', and everyone's feeling nostalgic. But this ain't no playground."

"It won't happen again," Edgar said.

"We swear!" Elena added.

I bobbed my head in agreement and tried to look innocent. Of course, if you've ever stood in front of a security guard while hiding a fortune-hunting, clue-holding metal cylinder in the top of your pants, you know that looking innocent wasn't easy. I kept my arms to my sides, covering the lump where the cylinder pushed up beneath my sweatshirt.

"Fine," Cy finally said. "But we're done. No more stories about your mom forgetting stuff." He arched a shaggy, white eyebrow in warning.

Elena practically tackled Cy with her hug. "Thank you, thank you, thank you!"

Cy patted her awkwardly on the back. "Can't say I ever been hugged after catching a hooligan before. . . ." He was smiling again. "Now you kids get a move on 'fore I change my mind."

We flew from Van Houten Toys and hopped on our

bikes. The sun had already set, its remaining glow fading in the west. As we pedaled away, the cylinder pressed against my side with every churn of my legs.

Elena veered off by the Elmwood High football field, and Edgar and I followed her. She stopped behind the bleachers, out of sight from the road. "Okay, Gee. What's in the tube thingy? I've gotta get home pronto, but I'm dying here!"

"You almost *literally* died," I pointed out. "I mean, really—Lady Elena, Warrior Scientist? What happened to being careful?"

Elena shrugged. "Even a warrior scientist's gotta celebrate."

I rolled my eyes and pulled the cylinder from the top of my jeans.

Under the light of Edgar's phone, we studied the silver tube. It was about twelve inches long, one inch in diameter, and flat on both ends. When I spotted a thumb-sized indentation near one end, I pressed it.

Click.

The end of the tube hinged open. Two items slid out—an old-fashioned brass key and a rolled-up sheet of paper tied with ribbon.

"Open it!" Elena urged, bouncing from foot to foot.

I kissed the paper for good luck and loosened the ribbon. Then—taking a long, slow breath—I unrolled Maxine Van Houten's final clue.

GINA: Kev—sorry. Didn't mean to miss your speech. It was Yankees Man's fault!

. . .

GINA: Hey, K! E and I should have told you where we were going Saturday but didn't want to stress you before big speech. Thought we'd be back in time. Super sorry.

. . .

GINA: K—I'm sorry we missed your speech. Don't be mad at Edgar. Was all my fault. But wait until we show you what we found today!

. . .

GINA: Kevin, I know I let you down yesterday. I wasn't a very good friend and you were right—you don't owe us anything. But the GEEKs aren't the same without you. Will you forgive me and give me another chance? We've got the final clue . . . AND A KEY! I know we can solve this with your help!

36

I lost track of how many texts I wrote to Kevin on Sunday evening, but I kept deleting each one before hitting send. I wanted to tell him how sorry I was. Wanted him to forgive me for messing up so badly. But apology-by-text felt too impersonal, and I wasn't brave enough to call him again.

I figured I could apologize the next day at school. I'd admit that Edgar and I should have waited and gone to Grove Park later. Kevin's speech should have been our first priority. After all, the newspaper had been at the Grove Park library since 1986. It would have still been there a few hours later. Once I apologized, I could convince him to rejoin our team.

Unfortunately, Kevin wasn't about to give me my shot at an apology.

He was nowhere to be seen when I got to school on Monday morning. At lunch, he sat by himself at a table along the wall. When I headed over to talk with him, he spotted me coming, picked up his lunch, and walked out of the cafeteria. I shuffled back to Elena and Edgar at our regular table.

As I set down my lunch tray, Sophina sauntered past. "Have the GEEKs finally surrendered the election?" She placed her hands over her chest in fake sorrow. Her nail polish of the day was bright orange with a sunflower painted in the middle of each nail. "At least poor Kevin finally realized how doomed his campaign was—even if his speech on Saturday wasn't *all* bad."

Edgar looked up at her in surprise. "*You* were there?"

Sophina shrugged. "Of course. You always have to keep an eye on your competition. Plus, I was hoping he'd make a giant fool of himself and I could capture it on video. I even brought a few kids from school. But his speech . . . well, we didn't hate it. All that stuff about there being lots of talented people here and working together to save the town? It wasn't the worst, I guess. I might even use a few of his ideas myself . . . after he *loses*." She flipped her hair over her shoulder and flounced away.

Edgar and I glanced at each other, then at Elena. We were both waiting for her to get angry. Make threats. Do *something*. Instead she just sat there and stared at the greasy slice of pizza on her tray.

"Elena, what's wrong?" Edgar asked. "Did you get caught sneaking home last night?"

Elena snorted. "Nah, that was easy. My parents weren't home yet, and my abuela was still watching TV, shouting at *Wheel of Fortune*." But then the smile slid from her face, and she started blinking rapidly. "But . . . when my parents got home, they said they'd been house hunting in Manchester. They found a place and want to make an offer because there's a job opening for my dad on the Manchester police force. It's not the chief job, but it's still more money than he gets in Elmwood."

I hadn't yet told my friends about Mom planning to take the job in Boston, but my own problem reflected in Elena's like the image in a broken mirror. I pinched the bridge of my nose. Of all of us GEEKs, Elena was the one who never gave in, never lost hope. But now . . . ?

"Come on. We have to solve this." I pulled out my notebook, where I'd copied down the clue, then poked Elena in the arm with my pencil. "I'm not letting you quit until you get to stay in Elmwood." *And I get to stay too*, I silently added.

Elena sat up a little straighter. "Is that a challenge, Gee?"

"Why? You scared?"

"Lady Elena, Warrior Scientist, is *never* scared." Elena picked up her pizza and waved it around like a floppy, rubbery sword. "Now stop yabbering and let's get to work."

We got to work.

> To find my final treasure
>
> You must build on all your gains.
>
> Where I felt the happiest,
>
> Now the last of me remains.
>
> Silent guardians keep their watch
>
> While music fills the air.
>
> The greatest gift awaits you—
>
> Just unlock the puzzle there.

"I looked up Maxine's obituary last night," I said, taking a sip of my chocolate milk. "There was no viewing, no casket. Her body was cremated, and her ashes were scattered by the waterfall in the preserve. Maybe that could be her 'remains.' But I don't see how those facts fit the second part of the clue."

"The music could be the birds singing?" Elena suggested.

But Edgar shook his head. "I don't think so. Remember how many kids used to play at that waterfall every summer? Someone would have found the treasure if it was hidden there."

"Good point," Elena said. "What about Maxine's statue in town? That's a part of her that remains."

I tapped my finger against my lip. "That's true!" I replied. "But . . . what about the music? And the silent guardians?"

I was hoping one of them would have a brilliant answer, but they both shook their heads.

I pulled out my phone to see if I had any new messages. After I had given up on texting Kevin an apology last night, I'd sent a picture of the clue to the whole group, including Max.

Great work, Gina! he had texted back. But then nothing.

The lunch bell rang. We were out of time for now. I sighed.

"Let's go to the Van Houten Manor after school," I said. "We can talk it out with Max."

Elena yanked hard on her braid. "My dad's picking me up straight from school now and driving me home himself. I'll have to wait for a chance to sneak out later."

Edgar coughed into his hand. "My folks told me I have to come straight home after school. The cows. It's deworming day." He grimaced. "Maybe tomorrow?"

I did *not* want to know what deworming day was. Regardless, clue hunting couldn't wait, and I had to make my friends understand why. "We don't have time to wait until tomorrow," I announced. "I didn't want to mention it before because I didn't want to think it could really happen but . . . my mom and I might be moving away too. She's already been offered a job in Boston. She only has until Wednesday to make her decision."

Edgar rocked back in his seat.

Elena spit out a bite of pizza. *"What?"*

"It's like with your dad, Elena—new job, new town. But with my mom, there's less than forty-eight hours to go. I can't waste twenty-four of them doing nothing." I tapped my pencil against my notebook. "I'll go to see Max and keep you guys in the loop."

I could tell Elena and Edgar didn't really like it, but they also realized I was right. Finding the fortune had turned into a real race, and I couldn't afford to stay on the sidelines.

"Okay," Edgar said.

"Fine, Gee." Elena took a bite of pizza. A line of reddish-orange grease oozed down her chin. "But if you find the treasure, you'd better share some of it."

When the final bell rang that afternoon, it felt like the start of the final fortune-hunting countdown.

37

After school, I rushed straight home to pick up Sauce. He tried his best to tug me toward the Maple Leaf, but after I produced a few treats from my pocket, he finally agreed to turn toward Van Houten Manor. The brass key jangled in my other pocket as I biked the familiar roads, Sauce trotting happily behind me.

Every now and then, I glanced around, keeping a lookout for Yankees Man, but he was nowhere to be seen.

I left my bike in the grass and ran up the steps to knock on the door. But there was no answer. I knocked again.

"Max?" I called. "It's me! Gina! I really need to talk to you about this clue."

Still, nothing.

I was alone. Was I the *only* one who wanted to find this treasure?

Sauce barked beside me.

"Sorry, boy," I said. "You're right. We're in it together."

I sat on the rotting porch steps and pulled out my notebook, figuring I would wait there for Max. I looked back through all the notes I had taken the last few days, hoping to "build on all my gains." But no answer magically appeared.

" 'Where I felt the happiest, now the last of me remains,' " I murmured to myself. I glanced up, my eyes landing on the family graveyard. I knew Maxine wasn't buried there, but it *was* full of remains. And she'd probably felt pretty happy here in the manor. Mostly, I had to do something, or I would go crazy.

So, "Come on, boy," I said to Sauce. And together the two of us went to check out some gravestones.

The little cemetery was dominated by the granite mausoleum. I shivered as I passed under its shadow. My eyes scanned the crooked tombstones and the fresh dirt where Alice Van Houten had just been laid to rest. Finally, my gaze landed on a statue in the far corner of the lot.

It was a stone angel, but as I drew closer, I realized there was something familiar about the face. It looked exactly like Maxine! The angel was playing a harp. Music! And the other tombstones of the Van Houten cemetery surrounded the memorial . . . like silent guardians.

Silent guardians keep their watch while
music fills the air. . . .

My heartbeat quickening, I looked at the base of the
memorial, where a brass plaque had been attached. It
read: IN LOVING MEMORY OF MAXINE VAN HOUTEN.

Now the last of me remains. . . .

Elena had been right about the statue of Maxine
being a part of her that remained. She'd just been thinking of the wrong statue!

"It all makes sense," I said, a smile spreading over
my face. "The treasure's right underneath my feet. I
know it!"

And I swear the corners of Maxine's stone mouth
twitched into the tiniest smile.

Sauce and I were running back to my bike when I caught
sight of Max. He was on the trail coming out of the nature preserve, headed for the manor.

"Max!" I called.

He looked up, startled. And I realized he was soak-
ing wet.

"Oh, Gina," he said. "Goodness, you scared me."

"Sorry," I said. "What happened to you?"

Max looked down at his sopping clothes. "Ah, I went for a walk. Needed to stretch the legs after being in the house all day, you know. I'm afraid I got a little too confident crossing a creek and fell in." He gave me a sheepish smile. "What are you doing here?" he asked. "Did you need me for something?"

I opened my mouth to tell him what I had discovered. I couldn't wait to see the triumphant look of pride on his face when he realized that I had solved the last clue. But then something stopped me.

If I told Max about the clue, he might want to start digging right now. And it wouldn't feel right to uncover the treasure without the other GEEKs. After all, we had started this together. We should finish it together too.

"I was just stopping by to see . . . to see if you had any ideas about the clue," I said.

Max sighed and shook his head. "I wish," he said. "But I'm stumped. I was hoping you might have thought of something."

"I might have," I said slyly. "But I need more time. I'll come back tomorrow after school with the rest of the GEE—of my friends."

Max gave me a thousand-watt smile. "Deal," he said.

Even as I smiled back, part of me wondered if there was another reason I hadn't wanted to tell Max that I'd solved the clue.

38

I thought about texting the other GEEKs when I got home that night, but I couldn't do it. I wanted to see the looks on their faces when I told them I'd cracked it. News like that really should be delivered in person, anyway.

Instead, I texted:

> Have something IMPORTANT to tell
> you guys. Lunch tomorrow.

But Kevin didn't show. In fact, I hadn't seen him at school all day.

"Kevin's not coming, Gee," Elena said when I got to lunch. "He's absent."

"But he's had perfect attendance since preschool!"

Elena shrugged. "He texted this morning and asked me to get notes and homework for him today. I think he nearly cried when I reminded him I don't take notes. So could you just hurry up and tell us what's so important already? I'm dying here!"

We huddled together and I told them about the memorial.

"But wouldn't it have been put up *after* Maxine died?" Edgar asked when I was done.

I frowned. "I guess so," I said. "But I bet she instructed it to be built to hide the treasure! Why would her family put a statue of her in the graveyard when there was already one in town?"

"Gee's right," Elena said. "It makes sense! The treasure's been at the Van Houten cemetery all this time . . . right where we started this whole hunt!"

"And after school, we're ending it," I said.

"I'm in," Edgar said.

"My dad's not picking me up from school today, so I'm in too," Elena said. "But I know he's planning to be home by four, so we've gotta be quick."

Kevin should have been with us too. But clearly he wasn't ready to forgive me or Edgar yet. Otherwise he would have texted us for our notes. And I couldn't wait another day. As Edgar would say, the show had to go on.

"My mom told me she was going to the Maple Leaf this afternoon and that she'd have Sauce with her. I'm supposed to walk him. Can we pick him up on the way?"

"Sure," Elena said. "Sauce is pretty much an honorary GEEK anyway."

And just like that, it was settled. After school, we hopped on our bikes and chugged over to the Maple Leaf.

As I plopped Sauce into my bike basket, which I'd fixed last night, all our phones pinged with a text from Kevin:

> I have something to show you. Meet me at Bamboozleland. 15 minutes.

"K-dog is back on the team!" Elena whooped, giving me and Edgar high fives.

I smiled with relief. Maybe Kevin *was* ready to forgive me. There was just one problem. "Yeah," I said. "Only we don't have time for Bamboozleland."

I bit my lip before typing back my reply:

> I'm sorry, Kev . . . but it's going to have to wait. We need you at Van Houten Manor ASAP. Please?

Edgar, Elena, and I zoomed to the Van Houten estate and pounded on the door. Max opened it right away, like he had been waiting for us.

"We know where the treasure is!" I blurted. "In the cemetery!"

"What?" Max took a step back. "But Maxine isn't buried there. She was cremated. Her remains were spread at the waterfall in the preserve."

For a second, I wondered if Max had been researching like I had, but then I realized he *had* probably been at Maxine's funeral. I remembered how he'd appeared on the trail from the preserve yesterday, sopping wet. Had he been searching on his own at the waterfall? After all, that's where I'd thought the treasure might be at first. *No*, I told myself. *He would have told us.*

"Yeah, but there's a memorial stone to her in the cemetery," I said. "She's playing a harp. Music! And she's surrounded by gravestones. Silent guardians!"

Max rubbed his chin, which had a couple days' worth of patchy stubble. His eyes lit up. "That may solve another mystery I came across last night." Max plucked a pink slip of paper from a side table near the door. "I found this invoice in an old file cabinet. It includes the bill for Maxine's cremation and memorial service *and* for a casket."

"Maxine was cremated without a viewing," I said. "She didn't need a casket."

"Exactly," Max said.

"I get it," Edgar said. "*Maxine* didn't need a casket, but maybe her *treasure* did!"

"Rah-oo!" Sauce barked, sensing the excitement in the air.

"Wait a second, Max-o-rama," Elena said. "You would have been at Maxine's memorial service, right? Do you remember there being a casket?"

Max blinked and looked at the pink invoice he was holding. "Well, of course I was there," he said. Then he smiled at Elena. "But I was quite young. Do you remember everything from when you were four?"

"Point taken," Elena said.

Max gave a double clap. "Now let's get to the cemetery and find this treasure!"

Right then, Kevin burst in through the door.

"You came!" I cried. My heart lifted. Kevin hadn't given up on us after all!

"Perfect timing, Kev!" Elena said. "We're about to score some loot!"

Kevin glanced from Max to us. He bit his lower lip. Maybe he hadn't given up on us, but clearly he still wasn't sure about Max. I fiddled with the brass key in my pocket.

"Come on, Kevin," I said. "I'm sorry for Saturday, but we need you now. *Please.* I really think we've cracked it this time. It should be all of us who dig up the treasure in the cemetery. *Together.*"

"The cemetery . . . I—okay," Kevin said.

I wrapped him in a hug. "I was afraid the GEEKs were done forever!"

Kevin stood rigidly a second, then hugged me back with one arm.

Sauce didn't want to be left out, so he licked Kevin across the kneecaps.

"Hellooooo," Elena said, waving her hands above her head. "Enough mushy friend stuff. I've got a four o'clock deadline here, people."

Kevin coughed and dropped the arm he was hugging me with. "Yes, I guess we should get to work. Especially since we're unsure of the depth of burial that needs to be factored in with the rate of soil displacement per minute."

Math genius Kevin was definitely back! I felt like whistling as Max led us out to the cemetery. The GEEKs were a team again. We were about to unbury a treasure that would save the town of Elmwood. And, best of all, we'd accomplished everything before my mom had accepted the job in Boston!

I shouldn't have counted our victory quite so soon.

39

Max grabbed two shovels from the porch as we headed toward the cemetery.

"I'll carry one," Kevin said, reaching for a shovel.

Max pulled the shovel back. "I've got 'em." He pumped the shovels up and down like he was lifting weights and gave a lopsided smile. "One in each hand keeps me balanced."

Kevin pursed his lips, but he didn't try to take a shovel again.

The angel memorial was in the far corner of the cemetery, and we headed that way. Just before we passed the weed-covered, stone mausoleum with the granite pillars, Max froze. "Wait! Did you see that?" He pointed with a shovel down the hill.

"I didn't see anything," Kevin said.

Elena squinted toward the woods. "Me neither."

Edgar and I both shook our heads. We all peered toward the edge of the preserve.

Max waved the shovel. "It was in the trees—a shadow, moving around. *Someone* is out there. Probably that guy from the library."

Edgar shivered. "Yankees Man . . ."

"Yeah," Max said. He tilted his head slightly toward the mausoleum, which was only a couple of steps away. VAN HOUTEN arced above the doorway in tall letters nearly worn away by decades of weathering. Above that hung a rusty bell. "When we pass the mausoleum, we'll be out of the sightline from the woods. We can slip inside and hide. Then when the guy comes, we'll catch him in the act. There're five of us. We'll have the advantage."

Kevin took a step back. "But if he's really—"

"Come on, Kev." Elena tugged him toward the mausoleum.

I pulled up a rusted iron latch and opened the mausoleum's thick, wooden door. "If we finally confront Yankees Man with Max around, we can stop looking over our shoulders all the time."

"But—"

"In you go." Max gave a nudge, and all four of us GEEKs crowded inside the stone building. As Max stepped into the doorway, he tossed one of his shovels aside. He snatched up Sauce by the scruff of the neck.

Sauce yelped. His stubby legs thrashed the air.

I stepped forward. "What are you doing? You're—"

"Shut up!" Max held the blade of his remaining shovel above Sauce's head. "One more step and your mutt goes bye-bye."

I wobbled on my feet. A chill raced down my body. What was going on?

"Set your phones on the ground and kick them toward me." Max's face was suddenly twisted and cruel, his blue eyes cold.

"But, Max, I don't understand." My entire body was shaking. "I thought—"

"Your phones!" Max swung Sauce from side to side. "Now!"

Sauce and I whimpered at the same time.

I felt Elena shift beside me. I didn't know what she planned to do, but I couldn't risk anything happening to Sauce. I blocked her with my arm. "Do what he says."

Elena grunted unhappily, but she set her phone down like the rest of us and kicked it to Max. It scraped and skittered across the mausoleum's tile floor, stopping by Max's feet.

"That wasn't so difficult, now, was it?" Max used one foot to kick each of our phones outside, not taking his eyes off us or loosening his grip on Sauce.

"But, Max—"

"His name's not Max." Kevin's voice was barely a whisper. "It's James. James Hatcher."

Edgar, Elena, and I all gawked at Kevin. He'd been mad at us for missing his speech, but he'd clearly been unable to resist doing more work on our investigation. Once a GEEK, always a GEEK, I suppose.

A horrible grin slid across Max's—*James's*—face. "Well done, Kevin. I'd applaud, but my hands are a bit full at the moment." James's knuckles whitened as he tightened his grip on the shovel. "Too bad you didn't put the pieces together sooner."

Kevin scowled.

My face flushed with heat as I thought about how I'd claimed we could trust Max—that he wasn't some bad guy, no matter what Kevin said. Obviously, Kevin had been right all along. And this time, my mistake was costing more than just a missed speech at the farmers market. I swallowed the lump in my throat. "But why?"

"And how?" Edgar added.

"And what about the yearbook picture?" Elena asked.

James Hatcher—a name that seemed vaguely familiar—smirked, clearly proud of himself. "Well, it was surprisingly simple to convince you kids and the rest of this Podunk town otherwise. You're not as smart as you think you are, you know."

"Our town's not Podunk!" Elena growled. "And neither are we!"

"Whatever you say." James shrugged. "Neither you nor your town was smart enough to realize that the real Max and I were roommates in boarding school. When I ran into Max at our recent high school reunion, he mentioned his aunt had passed away, but he couldn't get the time off to settle her estate. That made me remember the stories he'd once told about the lost family fortune, which got me wondering . . . what if those stories were actually true?"

"But we need that money," I said. "The *town* needs that money!"

James pointed at me with his shovel. "I need it more. I've got a bit of gambling debt. Never could resist a good bet, even back in boarding school. In fact, the real Max beat me in plenty of late-night poker games, which—of course—were absolutely forbidden at Grantwood Prep. The treasure can be Max's way of repaying me for his ill-gotten gains."

"Stealing a hidden fortune isn't the same as losing a few bucks to your roommate in boarding school!" Elena tugged her braid so hard, I thought she might pull her own head off.

"True," James admitted. "However, I happen to owe quite a large sum of money to a certain gentleman— I believe you call him Yankees Man—and he is becoming quite anxious for payment. In fact, if I don't pay him by the end of this week, he promised to put the *dead* in my deadline. So I'm afraid I can't afford to leave the Van Houten fortune to the town."

Elena's cheeks billowed in and out as she huffed angry breaths through clenched teeth. Edgar's usually rosy face looked pale. My eyes burned and I felt light-headed. Only Kevin—uptight, anxious Kevin—seemed calm, his dark eyes locked on James, his mouth set in a firm line.

"Naturally," James continued, "I didn't actually spot Yankees Man in the woods earlier. I do apologize for that minor yet necessary lie. However, I'd hate for him to show up while we're chatting, so I really must go. Thanks again for your help!"

James quickly stepped from the mausoleum and slammed the door.

The outside latch clanged shut. It was followed by a scraping sound as James jammed something in to bar the door.

The interior of the mausoleum was thrown into darkness, except for a sliver of light shining through a crack in the ceiling.

Elena, Edgar, and I threw ourselves at the door, thumping into it with our bodies. "Let us out!" Edgar cried. "This is kidnapping!"

A splinter stabbed into my hand as I pounded with my fists.

James's voice was now muffled by the thick door:

"By the time anyone comes along to hear you, I'll be long gone. You'll just be four crazy kids with a silly story no one will believe."

"Don't hurt Sauce!" I yelled.

Elena thrashed at the door. "When I get out of here, you'd better hope I don't have access to a particle accelerator and a fire extinguisher!"

The sound of our shouts and hammering fists bounced around inside the mausoleum's thick, stone walls. The only response from outside was a howl from Sauce and one final triumphant laugh from James Hatcher.

After a few more minutes of worthless pounding and shouting, we slumped against the door and slid to the cold tile floor. Sweat dripped down my forehead. My throat felt raw. My hands ached. "I'm so sorry, Kevin." I choked back a sob. "I should have believed you about Max—*James*—when you first said we couldn't trust him."

"Yeah, Kev," Elena said, "we should have listened to you."

Edgar nodded agreement.

Kevin slid down beside us. "I just wish I'd figured out a way to stop him. I thought there'd be more chances. I didn't realize he was evil enough to trap us in here." He turned to me. "After Saturday, I started digging some more." Kevin pulled out a piece of paper and unfolded it. "I found PDFs of all the old Grantwood Prep year-books on the school website. Check out the original caption on the photo of the robotics team."

I unclipped the reading light from my notebook and shone it on a familiar photograph. The caption was different from the one Chip MacDougal had included with the photo: *Max Van Houten (standing), James Hatcher, and Chip MacDougal with their entry for the Inter-Prep Battlebots Showdown.*

"That's why James Hatcher's name seemed familiar," I murmured.

Kevin nodded. "The caption with the photo online didn't mention that Max was the one standing. We assumed the names were listed left to right."

All along, I'd thought the photo proved we'd met the real Max Van Houten. I'd never considered the possibility that the man we knew as Max was actually one of the other boys in the photo. How could I make a mistake like that and still consider myself a journalist?

"Okay, so Max is James, and James is a jerk." Elena stood back up and kicked the door. "We can't just sit around. We have to get out, stop Hatchethead, and get the treasure for the town!"

"You're right about needing to get out," Kevin said. "But we can let James dig. He has no idea where the treasure is."

Elena stopped kicking the door. "What are you talking about, Kev? Of *course* he does! Haven't you been paying attention? The angel memorial in the cemetery? The 'silent guardian' tombstones?"

"I think that's wrong."

"But it all fits," I protested, "and we led James right to it. All he's missing is the key!" I plucked the brass key from my pocket and waved it around.

"Don't lose that," Kevin said, nodding toward the key. "I have a feeling we'll need it today."

"For what?" Elena said. "The treasure James is stealing?"

"Along with hunting down information about Max Van Houten, I also pulled up maps of Elmwood," Kevin said. "One of the maps was an aerial view of the town. That's when I realized Bamboozleland is a Bamboozler."

"Huh?" Elena, Edgar, and I all said at once.

"The *remains* of Maxine Van Houten aren't her ashes or her memorial or anything like that. What remains is her legacy—the Bamboozler. And Bamboozleland is laid out like a giant Bamboozler," Kevin said. "The paths and rides all lead to the spherical treasure in the middle—the carousel."

Edgar laughed. "So 'music fills the air' . . . that's the carousel music!"

"And the silent guardians are the carousel horses . . . ," Elena said.

"And somewhere on the carousel, we can 'unlock the

puzzle' by using the key." I slid the key back into my pocket. "I guess it makes sense that Maxine would have 'felt the happiest' at an amusement park instead of a cemetery."

"Now you GEEKs are catching on!" Kevin's smile shone brighter than my reading light.

Elena brought her hands to her face. "I can't believe you didn't tell us sooner!"

"He did try," I said sheepishly, remembering the text Kevin had sent telling us all to come to Bamboozleland. It was the second time Kevin had asked us to show up for him, and the second time I had put the hunt in front of our friendship. Maybe Kevin wasn't the one with his priorities backward. "I'm really sorry, Kev. You were right."

"It's okay, Gina," he said. "You were right too. About me being jealous. I *didn't* like Max giving you all the attention. I guess I have to learn to share the spotlight sometimes."

"Spoken like a true thespian," said Edgar proudly.

"Uh, speaking of 'Max,'" Elena said, "we've gotta get moving. We can't beat Hatchethead to the treasure by sitting around in here!"

Kevin's smile faded. "I know. But how are we going to get out?"

We started exploring the mausoleum's dim interior.

"Hey, here's an old candle thingy!" Elena swung a

282

long, wrought-iron candelabra that must have been used to light the mausoleum. "If Hatchethead comes back, I'll give him a smackdown."

"But he's bigger," Kevin said. "And he has a shovel, which is longer."

Elena lowered the candle stand. "Jeez, Kev. Let a girl dream."

"Wait, guys. Check this out." Edgar pointed to a rope coming from one of the crypts. It traveled up the wall to a pulley, ran close to the crack in the high, stone ceiling, then went out a small hole above the doorway.

I remembered the rusty bell I'd seen outside. "I've read about something like that. Some people used to be so scared of getting buried alive, they had ropes attached from their coffins to bells they could ring if they woke up."

"Ringing the bell would just get us in more trouble with James," Kevin said.

Elena studied the rope. "So I'll be careful not to ring the bell."

"What are you talking about?" I asked.

Elena hefted the candelabra in her hands. "Mrs. Garnsteen, third-grade science. Simple machines—pulleys, inclined planes, blah-blah-blah, and . . . *ta-da!*" Elena clanged the candelabra onto the hard floor. *"Levers!"*

Then Elena explained her plan.

The rest of us were skeptical. After all, Elena's recent climbing adventures had nearly gotten her killed. Twice. But we didn't have any better ideas, so we rolled with it. Kevin and I held the rope still so the bell wouldn't ring. Edgar gave Elena a boost. And Elena inched her way up the rope to the ceiling, somehow managing to wrap her feet around the rope and climb with one hand while holding the candelabra in the other.

At the top, Elena wedged the candelabra into the crack in the ceiling. Then—keeping her feet wrapped around the rope—she grabbed the stand with both hands and hung on it with almost all her weight.

At first, nothing happened. Then . . . *shrrrrk* . . . the stone in the ceiling began to move. The mausoleum brightened as the crack widened and more sunlight snuck inside.

Elena grunted and let even more of her body weight pull down on her candelabra lever.

Shrrrrk . . .

"Elena," I said, "be careful it doesn't—"

SHRRK!

The stone slid sideways. The lever popped from the crack, and Elena lost her grip. The candelabra plummeted toward my head. I let go of the rope and dove to the side.

Clang! The stand smashed into the floor, cracking the tile where I'd been standing.

Elena's feet saved her. As she flipped and dropped headfirst to the floor, she had the rope wrapped around her ankles. "Unh," she grunted as the rope yanked her to a stop. She bobbed upside down, dangling by her feet, just a few feet from the floor.

"Elena, are you okay?" I asked.

She gave a shaky laugh. "Saved by the bell."

"Saved by a *rusty* bell, apparently," Kevin said. "It never rang when you fell."

We hauled Elena upright and watched as she climbed back to the top. Her candle-stand lever had done the trick. The hole in the ceiling was just large enough, and Elena squeezed through and out of sight. A moment later there was a skittering sound as she slid down the roof, followed by a scraping sound as she unbarred the door.

Fortunately, the door of the mausoleum wasn't visible from Maxine Van Houten's memorial. After we slipped outside, Elena slid the shovel handle back into the door latch, which was how James had locked us in. "This way, he'll think we're still in there," she whispered.

We peered around the corner. James's back was toward us as he dug shovelful after shovelful of dirt from the base of the harp-playing angel statue. We needed to hurry. It looked like he'd already dug a couple of feet down. Eventually, he would figure out there was no treasure buried in that cemetery.

I spotted Sauce up by the house, tied to the porch railing. He was gnawing on a stick and looked surprisingly content.

Kevin noticed where I was looking. "We'll have to leave him," he said.

"No way!"

"We can't risk being spotted untying Sauce. Plus, if we take Sauce with us, James will notice him missing and know something's wrong."

"But James might hurt him!"

Kevin rested a comforting hand on my arm. "James has other things to worry about right now, Gina. He's not going to do anything to Sauce while he's focused on finding the treasure."

"Let's get the police," Edgar said. "Elena's dad can take care of everything."

"*No*," Elena said. "James was probably right—without the treasure, people will just think we're goofy kids with a silly story." She stuck out her chin. "And I'm sick and tired of my dad thinking that about me. I'm going to show him that sometimes *not* following all his rules can actually be a *good* thing."

We crept back to our bikes. I took one last, long look toward Sauce and whispered, "I'll be back, boy."

Then we pedaled like crazy toward Bamboozleland.

41

As we flew by Burkhart Bakery, Sophina and her minions were outside, handing flyers and cookies to passersby. Elena swerved onto the sidewalk and shouted, "Look out!"

Sophina jumped back. Her campaign flyers shot from her hands.

"Woot-woot!" Elena hooted as she blasted by.

I glanced back over my shoulder as we cruised away. Sophina's flyers drifted around her like fall leaves, a few landing in a mud puddle along the curb. She shook her fist. "You'll pay for that, GEEKs!"

We didn't slow down.

A few minutes later, we arrived at Bamboozleland. We stashed our bikes in some bushes and crawled through the hole in the fence. This time I knew—somehow just *knew*—we were at the right spot. We were about to find the Van Houten fortune. We were about to save Elmwood.

It didn't take long to get to the carousel.

Although the paint was now chipping away, and weeds grew up around it through cracks in the pavement, I could still remember how beautiful the carousel had been back when I was five. The brightly colored horses on their gleaming, golden poles. The polished silver organ pipes that surrounded the center column. The strings of lights that outlined the carousel's canopy, which was painted all the way around with scenes of Elmwood.

Kevin took charge. "Edgar, check the outer part of the platform. Elena, you and I will check the horses. Gina, check the center. There must be a trapdoor with a keyhole somewhere on this thing."

Even Elena didn't protest getting bossed around. We each started searching our area. Edgar hunted all around the outer edge of the carousel. Elena and Kevin examined the horses, Elena even climbing up to check for a keyhole where each pole poked into the canopy. I examined the thick column at the center of the carousel, the once-polished organ pipes now tarnished and dull.

We searched for five minutes . . . ten minutes . . . twenty.

"This is taking so long. . . . What if the treasure really *was* in the cemetery?" Elena asked. "What if Hatchethead found it and is escaping while we're messing around with a Bamboozler that isn't a Bamboozler?"

Kevin crossed his arms. "I know this is the right place."

"You *want* this to be the right place," Elena said. "There's a difference."

"But the clues fit!"

"Yeah, Kev. Just like they fit the waterfall and the cemetery."

While Kevin and Elena argued, I used my reading light to inspect the carousel more closely. I lay down and checked the bases of the organ pipes. I ran my fingers along each one. I even shone my light into the slits on the pipes where the sound came out. Which was how I found it.

At the back of one of the sound slits, there was a notch.

"I can't believe you convinced us a bunch of metal horses with bad paint jobs were 'silent guardians'!" Elena was saying.

Barely daring to breathe, I pulled the brass key from my pocket.

"Carousel horses make better guardians than tombstones!" Kevin argued.

I slid the key into the slit of the organ pipe. It caught for a second. Then I felt it slip into place.

"You know, Kev, I think—"

Click.

Elena's eyes widened. "Oh, sweet Einstein . . ." An entire panel of organ pipes swung outward, revealing a spiral staircase that descended into darkness. Elena slapped Kevin on the back. "I knew you were right, Kev!"

"But you said—"

"Gotta roll, GEEKs!" Elena said, charging through the door, which was the closest Kevin was likely to get to an apology.

I let Kevin and Edgar go in front of me and used my reading light to show the way. I really wished James hadn't taken our phones.

Our footsteps clanged on the metal stairs as we spiraled downward for about twenty feet. The air was cool, but there were no hints of dampness or decay. At the bottom, we huddled together, my tiny light barely strong enough to cut the blackness. I turned slowly, but my light couldn't reach the walls. Then its beam fell on a thin pedestal a few steps to our right. A single sheet of paper sat on top of the pedestal's flat, round top.

My Dearest Worthy Seeker & Discoverer,

CONGRATULATIONS! Since you are reading this letter, you must indeed be worthy of the trust I now place in you, for only a true lover of Elmwood could have made it this far. As I learned throughout my life—and as I hope you have learned, as well—two of the greatest treasures are knowledge and family. The material riches of this room are grounded in those two greater treasures.

My desire is that the riches of this room will provide knowledge of the past while inspiring new knowledge in the present, all while supporting Elmwood—my true family—through the ages. It will be up to you, the worthy seeker and discoverer of this fortune, to determine how those goals are accomplished.

With sincerest congratulations, best wishes, and hope for the future,

Maxine Van Houten

P.S. I don't think additional clues are necessary. Simply twist the pedestal.

All four of us reached for the pedestal at once.

We twisted it clockwise, and it turned smoothly

about a quarter turn before clicking to a stop. Suddenly, warm lights bathed the room, reflecting off polished brass walls that curved around us, as if we stood inside the center sphere of a giant Bamboozler. But . . .

"Where's the treasure?" Elena asked.

Other than the pedestal and Maxine's letter and the gleaming walls, the room was empty.

"Was it all a joke?" Kevin asked.

"Maybe someone already took everything," Edgar said.

Then a low hum filled the room, a single faint organ note. The curving brass walls slid slowly upward, revealing nooks and shelves and protective glass cases. The low hum faded away. The walls stopped moving.

We all stared in awe at the Van Houten fortune.

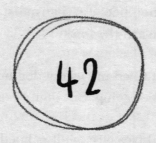

42

Edgar, Elena, Kevin, and I scattered around the room, bouncing from one treasure to the next, hollering our amazement at each new discovery: "A map of the constellations by Galileo!" . . . "A portrait of King Louis the Sixteenth painted before the French Revolution!" . . . "An unpublished work by Robert Louis Stevenson!" . . . "A SWORD BELONGING TO ALEXANDER HAMILTON!"

On and on and on, the entire perimeter of the room held priceless historical artifacts—hundreds of them—from all different time periods, all different places. We were like a bunch of kindergartners let loose in an ice cream shop without adult supervision.

When I found a glass case labeled MOVABLE TYPE FROM THE GUTENBERG PRINTING PRESS, 1450, I pulled out my leather-bound notebook. A journalist has to record things! Then I heard the bark.

"Rah-oo!"

Sauce? Relief filled me as my dog hurtled down the spiral stairs, tail wagging. But then I realized . . .

No!

The spherical treasure vault echoed with pounding footsteps. We froze, shocked, as James Hatcher barreled into sight.

James paused only a split second, taking in the curving brass walls lined with priceless artifacts. Then he dashed to his left, toward the glass case that held Hamilton's sword. In an instant, he had smashed the glass and withdrawn the sword.

"Hey! Put that back!" Edgar stepped forward and pointed at the label on the display case. "That sword belonged to Alexander Hamilton, hero of the best musical ever written!"

James leveled the sword at Edgar. Its golden hilt and slightly curved blade flashed. "Not another step."

Edgar stiffened.

James strolled back to the center of the room, blocking the staircase. He waved the sword toward where I stood, Sauce wagging at my feet. "Over there. All of you."

Elena, Edgar, and Kevin shuffled over, joining me and Sauce. None of us said a word, but I couldn't help thinking that we'd found the treasure without James's help, only to lose it to him anyway.

James scowled. "You know, I dug that stupid hole for what seemed like forever before hitting something. It was a casket, just like we'd thought, only it was small. Thought I'd found my fortune. But when I cracked it open, guess what?" He spat on the ground. "A cat skeleton and pet collar for *Otis*!"

Elena was the first of us to find her voice: "But how did you find us?"

James laughed—a nasty, cackling laugh. "Sauce is such a good dog!"

I glared at him. "Leave Sauce out of this."

"But, my dear Gina," James said, "he's the one who found you. After wasting my time digging up the memorial, I went back to the mausoleum. I'm sure you can imagine my surprise when I unlatched the door. But your dog—yes, good ol' faithful Sauce—has quite the nose. All I had to do was untie him from the porch, and he sniffed his way straight here." James smirked. "With a nose that valuable, I may even need to take that mutt with me when I leave."

I knelt and cradled Sauce to my chest. Even if his nose had worked against us this time, I'd never let James take him.

James kept his sword pointed in our direction and

scanned the room. "I would have preferred gold or jewels, but I do believe this will pay off my debts quite nicely. Might even have enough left over to buy a private island in the Caribbean. Wouldn't that be nice?"

A growl rumbled from Elena's throat. "You cheating, two-faced—"

"Last time, I tried to get rid of you the nice way." James's eyes narrowed. A sneer twisted his face. "I won't make that mistake again."

I pulled Sauce tighter to my chest. James had the only weapon, and no one knew where we were. The treasure vault had stayed hidden for decades, and if James trapped us down here, we'd never be found.

I drew a shaky breath, wondering if we'd make it out alive.

My eyes flitted around the vaulted room. Despite all the priceless artifacts, I didn't spot anything that could help us.

Which was when I realized that maybe the only way to bring down a con man was to con him right back.

I let go of Sauce and brandished my scuffed-up leather writing journal above my head like a sword of my own. "Check this out, James! An unpublished manuscript by . . . Mark Twain!" I started casually flipping pages. "How much do you think this'll be worth? A few hundred thousand? Millions?"

Rip!

I tore out a page and tossed it to the floor. "Oops." I smiled innocently. "I hope that didn't lower the value too much."

James bared his teeth. "Why, you little—"

Rip!

"Oops."

James lunged at me.

I hurled the notebook straight at his face.

It totally missed.

James laughed and raised his sword.

That's when Edgar blindsided him like a stampeding dairy cow. "In the words of Lin-Manuel Miranda's Alexander Hamilton . . . I am *not* throwing away my shot!"

The crunch of body on body echoed off the walls. The sword flew from James's hand and clattered to the floor. Edgar landed on top of him. James's head cracked against the floor, and his eyes glazed over.

Edgar scrambled up as Elena jumped on James's left arm. Kevin jumped on the right. Sauce and I settled across James's legs. Edgar plucked up the sword that had once belonged to Alexander Hamilton and placed its tip at James's shoulder.

James struggled, trying to free himself.

"Go ahead," Edgar said. "Try something. I had three fencing lessons for my role in *Twelfth Night*." He puffed out his chest, looking at least a little bit heroic.

Right then, new footsteps pounded on the stairs.

Had Yankees Man found us too?

A large shadow spiraled downward.

I tensed, ready to dive from James's legs and find a weapon of my own.

At first all I could see was the silhouette of a stocky man, his booming voice echoing around the vault: "Everybody freeze!"

For a moment, none of us could speak.

Then Elena broke the silence.

"Papá!"

I had never been so relieved to see Elena's dad.

Police Chief Luis Hernández's gaze swept the room, taking in the Van Houten fortune and Edgar holding a sword before finally settling on Elena. He sighed. "*Of course* it's my daughter. . . ."

"Papá, I can totally explain."

Chief Hernández rubbed his temples. "Maybe later." He nodded toward James. "For now, how about letting that man off the floor."

"But he—"

"I know." Chief Hernández pulled out his handcuffs. "James Hatcher, you're under arrest." He clicked one cuff onto the wrist of the arm Elena had pinned to the floor. Then he looked James right in the eyes and added, "And you'd better hope you didn't lay a finger on these kids."

As Elena's dad cuffed James's other wrist and pulled him to his feet, Officer Yang came down the stairs, followed by the last person I expected to see: Sophina Burkhart. I was still trying to figure out what Sophina was doing there when a third person—a tall, thin man I didn't recognize—appeared.

"Max!" Kevin exclaimed. "You made it!"

The stranger adjusted his glasses, smiled, and extended his hand. "You must be Kevin."

The next few minutes whipped by in a blur, but here are the basic facts:

FACT #1: Kevin had contacted the *real* Max Van Houten—an elementary school teacher—as soon as he'd figured out James was an impostor.

FACT #2: The real Max had come to Elmwood and gone straight to the police station.

FACT #3: After Elena made Sophina drop her campaign flyers in the mud puddle, Sophina followed us to Bamboozleland, then went to the police station to rat us out for trespassing. So she was there when the real Max arrived.

As Elena's dad led James toward the stairs, I waved my journal. "Sorry, it's just my notebook, James. A Mark Twain manuscript would have been a masterpiece." I tapped the side of my head. "Even a con man like you should have figured out we're GEEKs. And GEEKs would *never* destroy a masterpiece."

James growled.

Elena's dad kept a firm grip on James's arm, guiding him up the stairs and into another quiet Fair Valley afternoon.

Officer Yang, a disbelieving Sophina, and the real Max Van Houten trailed after them.

And there, standing together in the midst of priceless treasures, Elena, Edgar, Kevin, and I all looked at each other. And you may not believe me, but on my oath and reputation as a fact-finding journalist, I swear it's true—without planning or prompting, we all shouted the same two words at the exact same time: "GEEKs rule!"

EPILOGUE

Since you're one of the readers who followed my story, chapter by chapter, as I've uploaded it to our new *Elmwood Tribune* website, I suppose there are a few other facts you might like to know.

First, there's the town and the treasure:

FACT #1: The old North Star Bank building is being turned into a museum that will showcase all the masterpieces from the Van Houten treasure. It will also highlight the history of the Bamboozler and of the whole town of Elmwood. Naturally, the museum's souvenir shop will include plenty of Van Houten toys.

FACT #2: The Elmwood Theater is getting restored again and is scheduled to reopen in one month with an encore performance of *Our*

Town. Edgar convinced them to keep the hidden mirror on the wall behind the stage.

FACT # 3: The story of the GEEKs' treasure hunt has brought journalists, curious day-trippers, and—yes—other treasure hunters to Elmwood. Business is booming at the Maple Leaf, Burkhart Bakery, and other local shops.

FACT #4: Construction has begun on the new Maxine Van Houten Community and Nature Center in the preserve. It will include gardens, hiking and biking trails, and even a real swimming beach by the waterfall. Of course, the repaired Lookout won't be just for GEEKs anymore, but that's okay. . . . We're willing to share.

Of course, along with all the shops, there's also the *Elmwood Tribune* (and my mom):

FACT #1: Mom couldn't resist the chance to report the scoop about the Van Houten treasure, so she declined the job at Beantown Lifestyle Living.

FACT #2: The scoop about the treasure led to more newspaper sales, while having lots of readers of my online story led to lots of website hits, which led to lots of advertisers, which led to . . .

FACT #3: KEEPING THE NEWSPAPER RUNNING AND NOT HAVING TO MOVE!!! (GOODBYE, FINAL NOTICE!)

FACT #4: Last week, the *Elmwood Tribune* set a new record for total subscriptions, which broke the previous record set the week before.

FACT #5: Even though Mom turned down the job in Boston, Cousin Frankie had another connection. Mom now has a monthly column in the *Boston Globe*—"Letters from Elmwood." Apparently, city slickers enjoy regular doses of small-town life, especially after the whole treasure adventure put us on the map.

FACT #6: Mom's first "Letters from Elmwood" column included an interview with Ms. Kaminski about her experiences in Poland during World War II and the importance of rural libraries.

FACT #7: Mom's *next* column is going to be all about Bob Hensworth and the hidden fallout shelters of Elmwood.

I can't leave out the *real* Max Van Houten, who's actually a pretty good guy:

FACT #1: Max decided he liked Elmwood so much that he's moving here. He's going to help set up the museum, with some help from Mrs. Sánchez, who has been geeking out nonstop over everything we found. Classic librarian.

FACT #2: Max cleaned out his grandmother's old office and found plans for five new toys that were never produced. Production of the first new toy—the Jigsaw Jammer—begins next month. It's already trending on social media.

FACT #3: Van Houten Toy and Game Company is growing again, and Elena's mom and Kevin's dad got to keep their jobs. So no GEEKs will be leaving Elmwood anytime soon.

And speaking of the GEEKs . . .

FACT #1: Even though Elena got in trouble with her dad for all the top-secret treasure-hunting rule-breaking stuff, he *did* decide to let her participate in the science program after all.

FACT #2: Edgar's beloved Ollie was spared from the auction block. At least that's what Edgar says. (He's the only GEEK who can actually tell the difference between Ollie and rest of the herd.)

FACT #3: Sophina's plan to bring people to Kevin's speech to make fun of him backfired big-time. They ended up liking what he had to say so much that word spread around school and suddenly he was a whole new kind of popular—the kind built around a genuine desire to help the town. As a result, the vote for sixth-grade class president ended in a tie. Kevin and Sophina are now serving as co-presidents, so Kevin is getting a crash course in sharing the spotlight. Sophina (along with free doughnuts from Burkhart Bakery) has helped get other students excited about Kevin's latest idea: the Student Engagement, Readiness, and Volunteer Improvement Club of Elmwood (SERVICE).

And speaking of Sophina . . .

FACT #1: She's being treated as a hero for her role in the capture of James Hatcher. We GEEKs decided it was okay to share the glory and are glad that she went to the police, even if she was only trying to get us in trouble.

FACT #2: Sophina actually thought it was pretty cool when she found out about our treasure hunt, and we don't even fight with her (much) anymore.

FACT #3: Sophina's name starts with *S*. (Could there be GEEK*S* in the future? Stranger things have happened.)

The only other fact worth mentioning is that James Hatcher has pleaded "not guilty" to charges of identity theft, fraud, and kidnapping. But he *is* guilty. And the facts will prove it. Oh, and Yankees Man? He hasn't had the guts to show his face around here since Elena's dad took James Hatcher away in handcuffs. Our town belongs to *us* again.

Which is how the real story ends. At least, for now. You know, until my next big scoop . . .

ACKNOWLEDGMENTS

Handing out thanks at the end of a book is tough. There are so many people who help make a book possible that I'm bound to leave someone out. So, if you happen to read these acknowledgments and feel that you're one of those left-out people, you can write me an angry letter and just scribble *To T. P. Jagger* on the outside of the envelope. No stamp or mailing address is needed. Unless you're also enclosing cash.

My first and biggest thanks go out to my family, especially my wife, Amy, who has let me pursue my writing dream for more than twenty years. Thanks for believing I could do this and for making it possible to try. Also, thanks for reading all the books-that-never-quite-became-books along the way. Brace yourself. There will surely be more.

Thanks to Ramona and Lincoln for the many story ideas and inspirations you've provided simply by growing up. You're both in the book, so you might as well read it. (Yes, Lincoln, the fourth time *was* a charm. Now stop making fun of me.) Also, special thanks to my Bonus Child and Honorary Jagger, Caroline Lenore Malloy Diaper Wipe Scooby Snack Sciba. You always answer my random questions with gusto, and you never seem disturbed, even when I ask things like: "A man whose wife is dead keeps her favorite song as his ringtone. What's the song?" (Actually, now that I think about it, how worried should I be that you treat those kinds of questions as normal? . . .)

Thanks, Dad, for counting syllables and checking rhythm and rhyme. The poetic clues in this book are better because of you.

I've received plenty of great writing feedback over the years, but fellow authors Jan Gangsei, Amie Borst, and Pete Barnes have been my very own Big Three. Thanks for your continued willingness to read my stories and provide your insights. You're amazing writers and even better friends. You make my life *and* my stories better.

Additional thanks go to the team at Working Partners, with special shout-outs to Stephanie Lane Elliott and Ali Standish. I asked a lot of questions, and you answered every one. Just as important, if any of my questions made you roll your eyes, you hid your exasperation well. Thanks also go to the hardworking team at Penguin Random House, and especially to Diane Landolf for seeing the potential in this story and its GEEK-y cast of characters.

Finally, I want to thank all the fourth and fifth graders who came through my classroom in South Bend, Indiana, over the years. You enjoyed "The Misadventures of Flop and Spunky" just enough to make me believe I could actually, maybe, possibly write a book one day. And here it is.

Rumors are flying that the GEEKs are
treasure-hunting frauds. But when new clues
appear, the GEEKs have a chance to
clear their names . . . and win big!

TURN THE PAGE FOR A SNEAK PEEK!

The Elmwood Tribune

Friday, April 1

CEREMONY TO SIGNAL BAMBOOZLELAND'S RETURN

BY GINA SPARKS

Did you ever zip through the dips and drops of the Log Mill Run wooden roller coaster? Did you knock into other dinosaur riders at Bump-a-Saurus Wrecks? Or did you simply enjoy gazing across Fair Valley from the top of the Ferris wheel? No matter what your favorite Bamboozleland rides used to be, come out on Monday, April 4, and celebrate, because those rides are about to return!

The discovery of the Van Houten fortune in Elmwood last September brought much-needed tourism to the town. And the business community took notice! Soon Deepsight Development Enterprises purchased the Bamboozleland property, planning to restore and reopen the park. This additional source of income stemming from the publicity surrounding the fortune will provide a more significant, long-term boost to the local economy.

The entire town is invited to the ground-breaking ceremony at Bamboozleland amusement park. The ceremony is scheduled to begin at one o'clock in the park's amphitheater. See you there, Elmwood!

SIX MONTHS AGO, after my friends and I nearly got ourselves killed in a secret treasure vault hidden in an abandoned amusement park, I thought things would go back to normal. I'd return to being plain old Gina Sparks, freckle-faced and fact-loving journalist–the girl with a notebook in her hand and a pencil in her hair bun. My three best friends–Elena Hernández, Edgar Feingarten, and Kevin Robinson–would settle back into their normal routines. I figured the treasure-hunting excitement was over.

Man, was I wrong.

Really, the only thing that returned to normal was middle school lunch. The French fries were still soggy, the milk was still fresh from the cows at Feingarten

Family Farms, and—of course—Sophina Burkhart still couldn't leave us alone.

"GEEKs!" Sophina called, though not in the mean way she used to do before she and Kevin became sixth-grade class co-presidents.

I looked up from jotting notes in the leather-bound journal I always carry with me. I'd pretty much gotten used to the *GEEK*s label, but, well, it was kind of unfortunate that Sophina had figured out that putting the first letter of my name together with Elena, Edgar, and Kevin's spelled out *GEEK*.

Sophina sauntered over to our table, followed by her typical pack of minions—Kyesha Killman, Bella Ronelli-Compelli, and Mandy Sykes. Sophina's usually straight, shoulder-length blond hair had been curled on the ends and bounced with every step, and her lips glittered with pink gloss. She eyeballed us. "I must admit, you all clean up pretty well. Not as well as me, of course, but still . . ." Sophina patted down one of Edgar's loopy red curls and smoothed the collar of Kevin's polo shirt. I reflexively ran my hands down the front of my brand-new sweater, which my mom had given me as a special surprise that morning. "At least you look better than usual." Her eyes flicked over Elena, who wore a red hoodie with a cartoonish Albert Einstein on the front. "Well, *most* of you."

Elena scowled and tugged on her braid, which was

a sure sign she was about to launch a French fry at Sophina's head.

"Stay focused," she whispered to herself. "Bamboozleland. After lunch."

She loosened the grip on her braid. But her other hand twitched near the pile of fries on her lunch tray.

"Anyway," Sophina said, "I just wanted to stop by and tell you that when we get to Bamboozleland for the ground-breaking ceremony, you'd better not trip on the stage or anything. I don't need you GEEKs ruining my big moment. I heard Annalise Richardson from Channel 6 News will be there, so I figure I'll get a live interview." She flipped the ends of her perfectly styled hair and gave her best beauty-queen smile. "It will be my time to shine! Toodles!"

Sophina gave a tiny finger-wave and pranced off, her minions trailing behind her.

FACT #1: The special ground-breaking ceremony was to celebrate the soon-to-be redone and reopened Bamboozleland amusement park.

FACT #2: Bamboozleland was only getting reopened because *we* (the GEEKs) had saved Elmwood by finding the Van Houten fortune. So . . .

FACT #3: The GEEKs were being honored during the ceremony. But . . .

FACT #4: Sophina was *also* being honored, even though she hadn't actually helped find the treasure. All she'd done was call the police to come investigate, hoping to get us in trouble. The Elmwood chief of police–who happened to be Elena's dad–found us in the secret treasure vault, sitting on a bad guy.

As soon as Sophina was out of sight, Elena groaned and said, "Oh, sweet Einstein! That girl drives me crazy!"

Edgar shrugged. "At least she's nicer than she used to be. Thanks to her endorsement on the morning announcements, drama club's up to *four* members."

Kevin nodded. "Yeah, and she's not a bad sixth-grade co-president. My approval rating is higher than ever." He patted the tight curls of his high-top fade. "I know a lot of that is because we hunted down the Van Houten fortune, but it's also thanks to Sophina's support for my schoolwide calculator initiative. Ninety-five-point-two-four percent of sixth graders now believe we're doing a good job, and Gunner Bradley only disapproves because I wouldn't give him my strawberry Jell-O cup yesterday."

"Fine," Elena said. "You guys win. Sophina's not as annoying as she used to be." She crossed her arms. "But she's still annoying."

I kept quiet, but I knew none of us really had

anything to complain about. It wasn't just Kevin who was doing great. Edgar was pretty much a shoo-in to get the lead role in *Oliver!*, the first play scheduled for the newly renovated Elmwood Theater. Elena had started a YouTube channel where she shared crazy science experiments, and she'd topped fifty thousand subscribers after launching a video series called *Cool and Sometimes Dangerous Science Stuff You'll Never Learn in School*. And me? Well, thanks to my blog posts chronicling the GEEKs' search for the Van Houten fortune, I'd won the New England Youth Journalist of the Year award. That had given me a spot in the exclusive New England Journalism Mentorship Program, which included an all-expenses-paid two-day trip to New York City in July, where I would get to shadow a journalist from the *New York Times*. Incredible, right? I was still pinching myself.

But even with all that, I wouldn't have minded things going back to at least a *little bit* of normal. Sure, all the attention had benefits—it was way more fun going to school now that everyone liked us. But I was used to seeing my *name* in print, not my picture. As a journalist hunting for scoops, I found it tough to blend in and observe when everyone recognized me.

But a return to normal would have to wait, because right then the bell rang, signaling the end of lunch.

The cafeteria filled with the noise of sneakers

stampeding across the tile floor, trash being tossed into garbage bins, and excited voices calling out things like "Field trip time!" and "Bamboozleland, here we come!"

As we left the cafeteria, classmates gave us fist bumps and friendly "Hey, GEEKs!" as they headed for the school buses that would take us to Bamboozleland.

Gunner Bradley zoomed up and threw an arm across Kevin's shoulders. "Dude, this field trip gets me out of math class. Any day without fractions is a day I approve!"

Kevin looked so happy, he didn't seem to mind Gunner's poor view of math. As Gunner zipped away and bounded onto one of the buses, Kevin beamed. "One hundred percent sixth-grade approval rating!"

Edgar thrust his arms into the air in celebration. "As Shakespeare never wrote but should have—'tis a fine day for thou to be a GEEK!"

And, at that moment, it seemed like Edgar was right. But we would soon learn how quickly things could change.

BAMBOOZLELAND IS LAID OUT in a large circle, the paths like spokes in a wheel leading toward the carousel in the park's center, which is where we'd discovered the hidden treasure vault six months earlier. However, for the special ground-breaking ceremony, the park's center would have been too crowded, so the ceremony was being held in the amphitheater at the eastern edge of the park.

The amphitheater was a semicircle of crumbling cement steplike seating that descended in tiers toward a stage at the bottom. Schoolkids and townsfolk and news crews were settling in, waiting for the ceremony to begin. A microphone stand had been placed in the center of the stage, and a pair of large speakers faced the audience. A curtain hung from a steel frame along the back of the stage, and the other GEEKs and I gathered behind it.

Kevin smoothed the front of his shirt. "Do I look presidential enough?"

"Seriously, Kev?" Elena said. "You're the Elmwood Middle School sixth-grade class co-president, not president of the United States."

"I know," Kevin replied. "That's why I didn't wear a tie. Though maybe I should've worn a suit coat. It's kind of cold."

"It's mid-April in New Hampshire," Elena said. "What did you expect?"

Elena had a point. The sun was shining, but it was still barely above fifty degrees—a pretty typical early spring afternoon in the Fair Valley. I was glad for the fuzzy, extra-thick sweater my mom had given me.

While Kevin and Elena continued to debate clothing choices and the weather and Edgar hummed songs from *Oliver!*, I opened my notebook and plucked the pencil from my hair bun, ready to jot notes if I noticed anything newsworthy.

As I scanned my surroundings, I spotted my mom at the other end of the backstage area. She's the owner, editor, and do-it-all journalist of our town's weekly newspaper, the *Elmwood Tribune*. She and Kevin's mom were talking to two men. The first was a tall, thin, middle-aged man with glasses—our friend Max Van Houten.

The *real* Max Van Houten—not the con artist who'd impersonated him and almost swindled our town out of its finest treasures. Max had inherited the Van Houten Toy & Game Company after his aunt Alice had died.

The second man was a beak-nosed guy with perfectly groomed gray hair, dressed in a tailored black suit, complete with a baby-blue tie and matching pocket square. Thanks to an article my mom had written in the previous week's *Tribune,* I recognized him as Lambert J. Schoozer—the businessman preparing to restore Bamboozleland. Kevin's mom, who's on the Elmwood select board and was emceeing the day's ceremony, seemed to be listening intently. As Mr. Schoozer spoke, I saw her eyes widen and her smile suddenly waver.

I headed that way, my reporter radar pinging.

I'd only made it a couple of steps before I got attacked.

"Rah-oo!" A stubby-legged cannonball shot toward my kneecaps, long ears flapping.

"Sauce!" I knelt and let myself get tackled by my dog.

Sauce—part basset hound, part Scottish terrier—slurped his tongue across my face. I laughed as his long, Scottish-terrier mustache tickled my cheek. I was glad my mom had brought him. I figured Sauce deserved to be honored at the ceremony too. After all, it was Sauce's keen hearing and sense of smell that had kick-started our search for the Van Houten fortune in the first place.

I gave Sauce a quick scratch between the ears and stood up. "Come on, boy. Let's go see if Mom's getting a scoop!"

Sauce gave a happy bark and followed me.

I eased in behind my mom, eavesdropping on her interview. She held her phone out, recording Mr. Schoozer as he spoke.

"So," Mr. Schoozer was saying, "when we get done with it, Bamboozleland will no longer be just another tiny, outdated amusement park." He pointed across to the western section of the park, where an old wooden roller coaster called Log Mill Run climbed into the sky. "We'll tear down that splintering mess and replace it with the looping, lunging Space Spiral!" He gestured toward the center of the park. "Instead of a slow, boring carousel, our central attraction will be the Death Drop, where harnessed riders will plummet toward the ground, free-falling for over a hundred feet. And we won't just have better rides. We'll also expand, creating space for *more* rides. Bamboozleland will grow from a dud to a destination!"

Wait a second. . . . Grow? No wonder Kevin's mom had looked surprised!

It was my mom's interview, but I couldn't keep quiet. "Hold on." I stepped forward. "You just said Bamboozleland will expand. I thought the plan was just to restore the original park."

As a journalist, I knew I should have phrased that as a question, but I was too shocked to think straight.

Mr. Schoozer winked and flashed a white-toothed smile. "If a baby Bamboozleland is good, a big Bamboozleland is better! With all these woods around"—he swept out his arms—"the growth potential is phenomenal!"

I blinked, stunned. "But the woods are—"

"Excuse me." Mr. Schoozer held up a finger and pulled out his phone, which buzzed in his hand. He glanced at the screen. "I need to take this call." He turned his back and drifted away.

I looked at my mom, then at Max. "They can't expand!" I said. "The money from selling Bamboozleland was supposed to be used to buy more of the woods to extend the nature preserve, not the amusement park!"

"I know, Gina Bean." My mom put her hand on my shoulder. "Let's not worry about that right now, though." She smiled. "Today is a day to honor you and your friends."

"That's right," Max said. "If it weren't for you and Elena and Edgar and Kevin, we wouldn't even have an expanding Bamboozleland to worry about. For now, let's celebrate!"

I forced a smile. "Okay." I reached down and scooped Sauce into my arms, reminding myself of how bad things had been for Elmwood just a few short months before. "Mom, is it all right if I take Sauce to say hi to Elena and the others?"

"Of course, Bean. But be quick. The ceremony's about to start."

I hurried back to my friends, Sauce wriggling in my arms.

As Elena, Edgar, and Kevin scratched Sauce's head and got licked across their faces in return, I told them what Mr. Schoozer had said.

Edgar frowned. "I want Bamboozleland to be restored to the way it *was*–the way I remember it growing up."

Elena gazed dreamily toward the center of the park. "Not gonna lie–the whole Death Drop thing sounds uh-maz-ing. But still . . ." She sighed. "Not at the expense of the nature preserve."

"I don't know," Kevin scratched the back of his neck. "A bigger Bamboozleland would be good for Elmwood. More rides means more visitors, which means more support of local businesses."

Elena raised an eyebrow.

"I'm just saying there must be a way to make Bamboozleland bigger without cutting too much into the surrounding woods," said Kevin confidently. "In politics, you learn the art of compromise. Compromise makes it so everyone can be happy."

"Or *no one*," Elena mumbled.

Elena and Kevin can argue forever about almost anything–they actually *like* to argue. So I was glad when their Bamboozleland-versus-nature-versus-politics debate got interrupted by Kevin's mom calling out, "Okay, kids! Now's your big moment!" She stood at the edge of the curtain on the amphitheater stage, waving us over.

My heart pounded with an unexpected burst of nerves. I wasn't like Edgar, who loved the stage and the spotlight. Or like Elena, who confidently posted her science YouTube videos to tens of thousands of subscribers. Or like Kevin, who could stand in front of an entire gym of middle schoolers and get them fired up about building a school vegetable garden that would provide fresh produce to families in need.

I glanced around and spotted Sophina a little bit off to the side of our group. She was smiling and winking and snapping selfies that were probably uploading straight to Instagram.

I definitely wasn't like her, either. I was a journalist! I preferred being in the background!

I swallowed the nervous lump in my throat and gave Sauce an extra tight squeeze.

As I followed the others out from behind the curtain, my mom called out, "Go get 'em, Bean!"

"Hooray for our treasure hunters!" Max added.

I looked back at them and gave a tiny wave. That's when I noticed Mr. Schoozer. He was pacing back and forth, still on his phone, one hand waving wildly at nothing and no one.

He did *not* look happy.

YEARLING

Turning children into readers for more than fifty years.

Classic and award-winning literature for every shelf.
How many have you checked out?